IMAGATORIUM

BOBBY WAYNE

Bobby Wayne Fiction

IMAGATORIUM

Author: Bobby Wayne
Published by: Bobby Wayne Fiction
www.bobbywaynefiction.com
Copyright © 2021 by Bobby Wayne
Copyright © 2017 by Bobby Wayne Earlier Version 1-5297213981
ISBN 979-8-9853475-0-0 (Paperback)
ISBN 979-8-9853475-1-7 (eBook)

This is a work of fiction. Names, characters, places, and incidents either are the product of the author's imagination or are used fictitiously, and any resemblance to any actual persons, living or dead, events, or locales is entirely coincidental.

This book was printed in the United States of America.

Contents

1. The Church Gathering 1
2. Entrance Into Imagatorium 13
3. The Stronghold 36
4. The Sweet Aroma of War 92
5. The Descendants of Lot's Wife 155
6. The Easier Path 197
7. The Dry Valley 218
8. The Crowman 235
9. New Awakening 250

Closing 257

CHAPTER ONE

THE CHURCH GATHERING

A crow circled above a gathering at a church picnic. It was a warm summer day in the corner of a lonely country town. Next to where the people had gathered sat a simple little church. The paved pathway that led up to its front doors was cracked in several places.

Alongside the pathway was a fountain. It was enclosed by a barrier of shrubbery. A cemented baby cherub statue, with a leaf covering its privates, stood holding a large Bible over its head. The Bible also showed the wear of time, as did the cherub. Several cracks lined the streaked grayish image. The Bible was chipped at one of its corners. A spout of water spat from the Bible. The plaque in front read, "Living Water from the Word of God."

The fountain was meant to stand on its own as an artistic wonder. However, because of the vegetation and trees in the area, the fountain was often overrun by local birds, which loved to frolic with mischief in its pool. The dominant birds were a stubborn murder of crows that could rarely be shooed away when people were around.

The crow circling from above landed in the pool and joined the other crows on the fountain's edge. They all squawked at a little boy who ran by them on his way to a basketball hoop in the adjacent parking lot. The boy paid them no mind. He had a ball under one arm and a sketchbook in his other hand. His mother had just let him out of the car while she retrieved the potato salad out of the back. She yelled for him to slow down.

The boy was twelve-year old Johnathan Bismore. His dark curly locks dangled haphazardly around his head. He was a fair-skinned child of Cajun descent, or so he was told he might be. You see, Johnathan was an adopted child. It was only him and his adopted mother, Amanda, now. The passing of Amanda's husband from a prolonged illness was still fresh in Johnathan's mind.

To block out his pain, Johnathan always kept a sketchbook and pencil nearby to occupy his time. He tossed them next to the court as he shot baskets. At least he attempted to shoot baskets. He wasn't particularly good at it, but he was by himself and could not be criticized.

Amanda caught up to him as she headed for the tables where the others had gathered. She waved Johnny over. "Come on, Johnny."

Johnny took one more shot and missed. He grabbed the rebound, then went to swipe up his sketchbook. With the ball under his arm, he snapped his wrist back and forth as he jogged over to his mother.

Amanda waited for him to catch up to her. "I told you before, you need to stop popping your wrist like that."

"Sorry. It's just a habit."

"Well, break it. You'll get arthritis before you're twenty."

"Why did I have to come? You said I would be the only kid here."

"We went through this before. I was invited so you go where I go. Are you sure you don't have to go to the bathroom?"

He shook his head.

"OK. Just let me know if you do."

The picnic area was part of a large grassy lawn. Oak trees, mixed with stark evergreens, draped picnic tables nearby and spread beyond.

3

As Johnathan and his mother approached, three women were bustling about putting the food out. One of them was Edith. She was an attractive woman, pleasing to the eye. Her choice of clothing was often more revealing for her figure than it should have been. Today was no different. Edith's curvy allure was sometimes a bit much for a young boy of Johnny's age to be comfortable with. Her curly black hair contrasted with her smooth complexion and pointed features. She was in her late twenties. Johnny had heard from his mother that Edith had married a truck driver who was often away on routes to pay for her lifestyle and taste for "expensive proclivities," whatever that meant.

"Hi Amanda," Edith said as she reached for the salad that Amanda was holding. The others, who were preoccupied, waved, and acknowledged Amanda and Johnny's arrival as well.

Amanda smiled at them all in return and then handed the salad to Edith.

Edith winked at Johnny. "And how is my little champion doing? Are you still drawing?"

Johnny never understood why she referred to him that way, but it was not his place to ask. "Yes, Ms. Edith," he replied with a nod.

She pointed to his sketchbook. "Maybe I can see some of your drawings later?" She placed her hand on Johnny's back. He tensed inside but tried not to show it. "My, my, you're getting so big and handsome." Edith nodded to his mother. "The little girls at his school don't stand a chance, do they?" She laughed.

Amanda returned an uncomfortable nod, then guided him to the others. "Do you need help with anything?"

Setting down a bowl of barbecued beans was Daisy Blackwood. "No, I think we have it covered," she replied. "The boys are finishing up those burgers, and everything should be ready in a few minutes."

Daisy was the pastor's wife. She had a dominating personality that could be overbearing to certain people. One such person was the woman standing a few feet from her, Rose McCourt.

Rose was married to the local sheriff. In her own right, Rose's personality was just as overbearing. Daisy and Rose's husbands had achieved a certain level of importance in the town, one being the town's pastor and the other the town's sheriff. Their dislike of each other was obvious to Johnny. Of course, their interactions were masked with saintly etiquette and acceptable Christian jargon.

After Daisy set the bowl down, Rose raised her brow and repositioned the bowl more to the center. Daisy rolled her eyes and grabbed the paper plates. "And where would you like to put these?" she asked, barely able to hide her annoyance.

"Right here, dearie," Rose replied, pointing to the spot where Daisy had previously set the bowl.

Johnny's mother confirmed to him one day that Daisy hated it when Rose called her "dearie." To Amanda, it was disrespectful to address the first lady of a church as such. Johnny wondered why Rose did it anyway.

Rose took the potato salad from Edith as well and placed it where she wanted it to be.

Daisy plopped the paper plates down not so gently. Rose smirked. Daisy stomped toward her husband, Pastor Jason. The pastor and Ken, the minister of music, were approaching with an ice chest filled with soft drinks and bottled water.

Ken was an African American man in his thirties who had a kind personality and an effeminate demeanor. He got along with everybody whether they liked him or not. They set the ice chest down at the other end of the table.

"Is there anything else you need, Pastor?" Ken asked.

"I think we can handle it from here. Thank you." Pastor Jason took pause to look at the crows flying over them. "Well, Amanda and her boy are here. So, I guess that's it. Why don't you see how Ezekiel is doing with the rest of the burgers. We're almost ready to eat."

"Will do, Pastor," Ken replied, waving his hand limply down from the wrist. He nodded to Daisy before departing. Daisy forced a smile in return. It was apparent to Johnny that Daisey wasn't fond of Ken either.

Pastor Jason walked over and kissed his wife on the cheek. They whispered to one another. Johnny noted from Daisy's body language that she was upset about something. He figured that she was complaining about Rose.

Their attention was interrupted by Edith, who had turned on the radio from her portable stereo. The music coming out was from an oldies station, or so it sounded to Johnny. She closed her eyes and bobbed her head, snapping her fingers to the music. "I used to love this song when I was a teenager. It reminds me of the time... I was the head cheerleader in high school. I was over many girls, and a lot of boys swooned over me. I would smile, bat my eyes, swing my hips, and do other things to get what I wanted." She sighed. "I'm saved now, but those were the good ol' days."

"Maybe changing to a Christian station will be more appropriate for this setting," Daisy said.

"Yes, you're right," Edith replied, nodding. "I have some soft Christian music here." She switched to pre-recorded music. As the music played, she looked up. "How's that?"

"It's perfect, Edith," Rose interjected, although the question was directed to Daisy.

"Thank you, Edith," Daisy replied.

"Honey," Pastor Jason said, "why don't we go check on Ezekiel and the burgers on the grill?" He waved to Johnny. "You want to come with us?"

Amanda motioned for Johnny to go. He put the ball down. Amanda reached for his sketchbook, but Johnny held it tight and shook his head. Then he followed them over to the grill area.

As they approached, Ezekiel and Ken were engaged in conversation. Hearing the sizzle of meat, Johnny took a whiff of the hickory smoke. Zeke, as he was called, had just flipped a few burgers, and dabbed some barbecue sauce on them. He was an older woodsy-type man with a grey beard. He was balding on top of his head, and the hair he did have, on the sides, always seemed in need of combing. He reminded Johnny of a homeless Santa Claus, though with a shorter beard.

"Come on Zeke," Ken argued. "I've heard you sing before. You have a wonderful bass voice. The church needs you."

"It's not my gifting. I have no desire to do it, I tell you." Ezekiel scooped his spatula underneath a burger and placed it in the pan of meat next to him. He poked at another to check its readiness.

Ken looked up and shrugged at the pastor. "I'm trying to convince Zeke to join the choir, but he won't budge."

"That's a wonderful idea," Pastor Jason replied. "We could use some more men to volunteer and serve."

Daisy nodded without smiling.

Ezekiel waved his spatula. Johnny imagined he was waving it like a weapon, about to command an army. "When it's time to sing the hymns, I'll do my part like everybody else. Otherwise, I like to work on cars, put things together, and flip burgers." He put the last of the burgers into the pan. "That's what I enjoy doing." He nodded to the array of meats inside it. "Well, these are ready. I suppose we can start whenever you want to, Pastor.

"I'll take them over to the table," Pastor Jason replied. He lifted the pan of meat and proceeded to carry it back.

They followed him. As they reached the tables, Pastor Jason called for everyone to gather for the blessing.

Rose made a special space for the meat. Edith silenced the music. They gathered in a circle for Pastor Jason to pray a blessing over the food, holding hands and bowing their heads. "Dear Heavenly Father," he began, "we thank you for this gathering in fellowship. Let us sharpen and grow one another, resisting the devices of evil. We pray a blessing upon all the families represented here today as well as the entire congregation. We also pray a blessing on the food we are about to eat to the nourishment of our bodies. In Your name we pray."

After the blessing, they all got their food and drinks, then sat around the tables to eat. Johnny sat between his mother and Ken. Since Johnny was the only child there, the adults talked around him. This was fine with Johnny. He preferred to eat quickly and then go off by himself to draw. He set his sketchbook on the table next to his plate.

After some general conversation, Ken nodded to the sketchbook and tried to include Johnny. "So, I understand you're an artist?"

Johnny shrugged. "I like to doodle around."

"You mind if I see?"

Johnny was normally guarded about his drawings and doodles, but there wasn't much in this sketchbook except a couple of drawings. The rest were half sketches and notes, although he thought the work inside was pretty darn good. Johnny let his guard down and offered the sketchbook to Ken.

"You should feel honored," Amanda said. "He rarely shares his drawings with me."

Johnny started to protest by saying that, besides buying the occasional sketchbook, she had never shown much interest, but he held his tongue.

Ken opened the sketchbook to a detailed sketch. It was the face of a dragon. "Hey, that's pretty good." Ken turned the page to a picture of a black bird on the branch of a tree. He nodded in approval. The final drawing was a bunch of bat-type silhouettes fluttering over a man seated in a chair. On the opposite page was a skeleton holding a spear and a shield. "Now that is interesting."

Amanda leaned over to look. She frowned. "I don't know why you draw such things, Johnny. I mean, can't you draw something beautiful, like flowers or something?"

"He has talent," Ken replied. "I'm sure he could draw something like a flower."

"Yes, a flower," Daisy said. "Like this pin on my lapel."

"I suppose I could," Johnny replied.

11

"Or a red rose," Rose interjected. "There's nothing more majestic than a red rose."

"A flower? Bah!" Zeke shot Ken a glare. "He's a boy. Let him draw dragons."

Amanda shot him a look. Zeke turned away sheepishly.

Johnny took his book back from Ken and then turned to his mother. "May I be excused?"

Amanda looked at his nearly full plate. "You've barely eaten."

"I'm not that hungry."

Amanda nodded. He walked over to put his cup in the trash.

"I hope we didn't upset him, Amanda," Ken said.

"No, he likes to go off by himself and draw. He's the only kid here and is probably not interested in our adult conversation. He'll be fine."

The others nodded, and within a minute or so had changed the subject.

Johnny turned to look back at his mother. She watched him with concern in her face, then forced a smile. Wanting his privacy, he turned and walked off toward one of the nearby trees.

Chapter Two

ENTRANCE INTO IMAGATORIUM

"Rabble, rabble, squawk and babble in whisper's ear, scrabble, scrabble"

Johnny took his sketchbook and sat against a nearby Oaktree. He wanted to get away from adults trying to pry into his private sanctuary. Drawing helped him get away. Johnny yawned. He shut his eyes for a moment and then opened them again. He looked up at a rigid branch that bore a cluster of leaves. Then he opened the sketchbook and began to doodle. After all, doodlers do what doodlers do, and that was to doodle. He shaded in one of the leaves, looked back up, then yawned again. He felt relaxed. The tree behind his back comforted him. He didn't know why he was so tired, but he was.

As he looked up at the tree, he was astonished to see a bird land on one of its branches. It was an odd bird, a raven of sorts, and of unusual color. Its bright orange feathers nestled firmly on its frame. Its proud black beak was slightly arched. It tilted its head toward Johnny and squawked.

Johnny had never seen anything like it. He looked back at the picnic area where the adults were still conversing. None of them paid him any mind. Johnny turned back to the orange raven.

"Squaaawwk... rabble," it said. "Rabble, rabble, rabble..."

"Rabble?" Johnny repeated.

"Rabble, babble, rabble, squawk... Johnny..."

Johnny chuckled. "You're talking? You know my name? You're a talking bird."

"SHHHHHhhhhhhhhhhh...," the bird whispered way longer than a normal shush. It shifted its claws on the perch and lowered its head toward him. "Johnny, Johnny, Johnny," it whispered as it bobbed its head. "Johnny, Johnny, Johnny," it repeated with ever-increasing volume. "Johnnnnnnyeeeee!" it finally sang out with a sustained melody.

Johnny laughed. He looked back again to see if anyone had heard it. No one had. "You're a very odd bird."

"Squawk, squawk... I know secrets."

"A talking bird that knows secrets. That's doubly odd, I would say."

"SHHHHHhhhhhhhhhhh..."

"What kinds of secrets?"

The bird squawked and blinked. "Your secrets," it whispered. "Johnnnnnnyeeeee," it sang out once again.

"How do you know my secrets? I've never come across the likes of you, or I would have remembered."

"Squawk, squawk... rabble, rabble, babble..."

"There you go again with the rabble babble."

"I know other secrets too."

"I think you're bluffing. You're a babbling, bluffing bird."

"Squaaaawkkkk! That's not nice, not nice at all."

"Well, I don't mean to be 'not nice.' It's not every day one talks to a bird."

"Squaaawkkk, squawk, rudeness, just like the lady!"

"I'm not rude; you're being unfair," Johnny said. "Pure gibberish," he said under his breath, repeating a term he had heard his mother use.

"SHHHHHhhhhhhhhhhh..., Johnny is rude," the bird whispered.

"And what lady?"

"Squawk... Rude, rude, rude," the bird repeated with a lower voice. "Rabble babble scrabble..."

Johnny rolled his eyes. "Rabble babble..."

"Follow me, and I will show you secrets," the bird said.

"Follow you too where?"

The bird spread its wings and squawked. It flapped its wings and flew off toward another tree, further away from the picnic area. Caught up in the moment, Johnny set his sketchbook down and followed. "Wait, where are you going?"

The bird did not respond, merely perched on the next tree and waited for him to catch up. When Johnny came near, the bird took off again.

"Wait!" Johnny yelled, chasing after it.

After a time, the bird landed on a big rock, which was about the size of a two-car garage. It squawked. It paced, waiting for Johnny. "You have to keep up if you want to see secrets."

Johnny stopped to catch his breath. He bent over and put his hands on his knees. "Well, maybe I shouldn't be following a talking bird to who knows where."

"SHHHHHhhhhhhhhhhh... rabble, rabble."

As Johnny eyed the bird on the rock, he realized he had never seen that rock before. It was a sizable landmark that he would have recognized in such a small town. He looked back at where he thought the picnic area was. There was nothing but an open plain with some distant trees. There was no church, no roads, and no people.

"Where am I?" He looked around nervously. Thinking he should retrace his steps, he took a step in one direction and looked toward another. He had no recollection of how to get back. "Hello, anybody out there? Mom?"

"Shhhhhhhhhhh," the bird whispered. "They might be around. They will tear you apart. Squawk..."

"Stop that! Don't shush me. You're a deceptive bird. Take me back right now!"

The bird paused for a moment before responding. "I can't take you back, but the lady can."

"What lady?"

"I'll take you to her. You will see secrets."

"I don't want to see secrets. I want to go back."

"Rabble, rabble, squawk, and babble... In whisper's ear scrabble, scrabble."

"That's nonsense."

"Come on, Johnnyeeee, squaaaawk. It's right behind this rock."

"Why should I trust a nonsensical bird? Who are you?"

The bird blurted out his annoying squawk once again. Johnny sighed deeply in response. The bird shuffled toward him. "Nimoy," the bird said. "I'm Nimoy."

"Nimoy."

Nimoy expanded his wings and lifted himself in the air. He circled around Johnny and flew to the other side of the rock. "Follow me, Johnnyeeee," he said, his voice trailing off as he disappeared from sight.

"Wait!" Johnny ran after the bird, but when he came to the other side, he stopped abruptly. Before him stood a beautiful black door with golden trim. On the door was a golden handle. The unusual part about the door was that it stood there by itself; it was not attached to anything. Next to it was a small tree which hung a single piece of fruit. Nimoy perched himself on one of the tree's branches. Behind and around the door was open land. Johnny wondered how the door was able to stand there. He peeked behind it and confirmed that nothing was there. It was just a door in the middle of nowhere.

He looked at the bird. "What's the use of a door when there's nothing behind it to let you into?"

"Squawk... The lady is inside."

"Inside where?" Johnny asked. "There's nothing behind the door."

"SHHHHHhhhhhhhhh inside," the bird whispered. "Eat the fruit, the fruit, the fruit, the fruit."

Johnny walked up to the fruit dangling from the tree. The more he looked at it, the more colorful and pleasing it appeared. It was a combination of red, orange, and green. It seemed to increase in richness and color the more he looked at it. Johnny could smell the tangy sweetness of its scent.

"The fruit, the fruit, the fruit..."

The stem holding the fruit gave way as Johnny pulled it toward him.

"Squawk!" the bird repeated. "Eat the fruit, the fruit, the fruit, rabble, babble, scrabble."

A swirling glow whisked around Johnny's hand, beckoning him to partake. Johnny surrendered to his desire and bit into it. Its juices dribbled down his chin and onto his shirt. Johnny closed his eyes with delight. It was the sweetest thing he had ever tasted.

"You did it now!" the bird said. "Here we goooooooo!"

"What are you babbling about now—" His voice was cut off by a rushing sound. The ground shook, and the door flung open, unleashing a dark whirlwind. The pressure from the swirl lifted Johnny off the ground.

Johnny cried out as he and the bird were sucked inside. Nimoy squawked repeatedly. Their voices faded away. The door slammed behind them and disappeared into nothingness.

Johnny was drawn forward into the dark faster than he thought was humanly possible. He yelled out but then succumbed to the fear that he would smack into something. Speeding lights streaked past him. He could not make out what they were, outside of flashes and blurs. He no longer could hear Nimoy's squawking. He could only hear the pattern to his breath and the rhythm of his heartbeat. He felt lightheaded. As he looked forward, he saw a small singular light growing ahead of him. It did not flash by him like the rest. The closer he got to it, the larger it grew. He was mesmerized by the light. At the same time, he felt himself drifting out of consciousness. The light engulfed him, and Johnny passed out.

The next sensation that Johnny felt was engulfing comfort. He felt relaxed as if he were lying on a pillow of cotton. He heard chatter and squawking around him. However, he also heard another voice, the warm voice of a woman. She was close to him.

"He'll be fine," the woman said.

"Squawk, squawk, he doesn't look fine," a deep, husky bird voice replied. "Rabble, rabble."

"Squawk... are you sure that's him?" another bird asked.

"That's him. That's Johnnyeeeeeeee," Nimoy sang out with a melodic rhythm.

"I told you he'd come," the woman said.

"Squawk...I brought him here, remember?" Nimoy protested.

"Yes, you did. Thank you, Nimoy," the woman replied.

"Well, he's a scrawny boy," the deep, husky bird voice squawked.

Johnny's eyes were heavy. He blinked them open and tried to focus. Everything was a haze, but from what he could determine, he was on a grassy field with leafless trees all around. Sitting next to him, with her legs folded, was a beautiful woman. Her light olive skin appeared smooth, and her brown hair was woven into a long braid behind her. The woman was wearing a white summer dress and a matching hat that flopped ever so slightly over her face. "Wha... Where am I?" Johnny asked.

"Take your time, Johnny," the woman said. "It may take you a few minutes to adjust to the atmosphere here."

Looking just beyond her, Johnny saw three birds perched on a tree--two black birds, one bigger than the other, and Nimoy. The bigger bird was a crow, and the other was a raven. Feeling woozy, he took a moment to orient himself.

Meanwhile, the birds continued their chatter. "Babble, babble," the black raven said. "How is he going to handle a sword? Squawk! I heard he doesn't have a lot of friends."

"Rabble, rabble," the bigger bird said. "What do you expect? His father got sick and died. Terrible that is, just terrible."

"Turrible," Nimoy replied.

"Scrabble, babble, which father?" the black raven asked. "He's adopted, you know," he whispered.

The bigger bird made a clicking noise. "The one that the child knew, stupid," he replied. "Scrabble, scrabble..."

"Turrrrible," Nimoy repeated.

"Be quiet," the woman said. "You'll ruin everything. It's wrong to chitter-chatter regarding things you should keep quiet about. It's gossip."

The black raven squawked and chuckled. "Ha ha... babble, babble. We like it!"

"Rabble, rabble... Yes, we like it," the bigger bird echoed. He made a clicking noise. "And such is the way of the crow."

"Gossip is sooooo delicious!" Nimoy said. "It's like a tasty morsel, better than the fruit, the fruit, the fruit." As he repeated the words, he danced on the branch. "The fruit, the fruit..."

"The fruit, the fruit!" The other birds joined in, with Nimoy's encouragement.

Johnny had had enough of the babbling birds. "You know I can hear you, right?"

"SHHHHHhhhhhhhhhh," Nimoy replied. "We know secrets," he whispered.

"Really," the woman said. "Why I even tolerate you three is beyond me. Such babblers they are, Johnny. Pay them no mind. You'll get caught up in their nonsense and spread things you don't even know."

"Rabble, rabble," Nimoy said in a mocking tone.

"Babble, babble," the black raven replied.

"Such pretentious tomfoolery," the woman said.

The birds laughed and squawked.

"Rabble, rabble, squawk, and babble," Nimoy replied. "So rude you are."

"Yes, rude. Rabble, rabble," the black raven said.

"Babble, babble," the bigger bird squawked.

"Secrets!" Nimoy sang out.

The woman rolled her eyes and made a gesture around her own head. "Yes, yes... rabble, rabble, squawk, and babble, in whisper's ear, scrabble, scrabble." She repeated the words to herself over and over again. "Rabble, rabble, squawk, and babble, in whisper's ear scrabble, scrabble."

The birds began to dance and sing again. They too repeated the words over and over, although Nimoy kept mixing them up.

"Excuse me," Johnny said, sitting up.

"Rabble, rabble, squawk, and babble, in whisper's ear scrabble, scrabble," the woman repeated.

"Squawk, rabble, rabble," the birds continued. Nimoy turned and began shaking his tail feathers in dance.

"Excuse me," Johnny said again, raising his voice.

The others ignored him as they continued their nonsensical babble.

"Stop it!" Johnny yelled.

"Oh my," the woman said, placing her hand on her chest.

The birds all stopped. Nimoy shuffled his feet around from his perch to face him. "So rude," he huffed. "Just like the lady."

"It figures," the bigger bird said.

The woman shushed the birds to let Johnny speak.

"I'm lost. I want to go home."

The woman looked at him intently. She put her hand to her chin and scrunched her lips together. "Hmmm... that sounds important."

After a momentary pause, the bigger bird spoke up. "E.T. phone home?"

The other birds all joined in with squawking and laughter at the bigger bird's joke.

"Maybe he's an alien!" the black raven cried. "Babble, babble..."

"If he is one, she must be one too," Nimoy said. "Rabble, rabble..."

"OK, OK, knock it off. He's serious," the woman said, smiling coyly. "He must be frightened." She turned to Johnny and pooched her lips. "Are you frightened, Johnny?"

Johnny held his head down. "Well, no, I'm just in a strange place, and I want to get back. They'll worry about me if I don't get back." He stood and brushed himself off. Out of nervous habit, Johnny began snapping his wrists.

The woman nodded to him. "You know you really shouldn't do that to your wrists, Johnny."

Johnny rolled his eyes, "I know, I know..."

"They won't worry about him," the black raven whispered.

"They probably don't even know he's missing," the bigger bird added.

"Pooorrrrrr Johnny," Nimoy said. "They don't want you."

"The orange bird told me that a lady would be able to show me the way back home. Are you the lady he was talking about?"

The woman held out her hand to shake his. "My name is Lenore." She waved her hand at the birds. "You've met Nimoy. The big crow is Chinwag, and the other there is Mr. Buggins."

Chinwag squawked.

"I like bugs," Mr. Buggins said.

"Where am I?" Johnny asked. "What is this place?"

"Imagatorium," Lenore replied.

"Imagatorium? What does that mean?"

"It doesn't mean anything, Johnny. It's just where we are."

"Can you... I mean, can you show me the way home?"

Lenore rose to her feet and stretched her arms out wide. "Well, that may not be as easy as it seems." She twirled in a circle to where the birds were. Her dress expanded to the shape of a turning bell and collapsed to a stop when she did. She struck a pose. "And as it seems may not be that easy."

Johnny looked at Lenore, somewhat confused. "Isn't that the same thing?"

Lenore stepped toward him and poked him on the shoulder with her finger. "Yes, Johnny. Yes, it isn't."

"So, you can take me home?"

"Well, I suppose I can. Yes, I will!" she said with exuberance. "You see, Johnny, you have to go out the way you came in. But the Great Door doesn't stay in one place for long. You never know when it will appear or disappear. That is, except for one place where it returns for hours on end. It's a place just above the great valley to the north. Yes, I will show you the way."

"Squawk, dangerous," Nimoy hummed.

"How long will it take to get there?"

"Oh, a few days," Lenore replied, "or maybe a few weeks. I don't know. It may only take a few minutes. What is time anyway?" She laughed. Then she turned and began to skip away, waving for him to follow. "Come this way, Johnny."

The birds squawked and left their perches to fly after her. The birds circled and squawked around them as Lenore skipped along and Johnny followed.

"Is this the way to the great valley?" he shouted.

"No, of course not!" she yelled back. "We have to get the sword first!"

"The sword?"

"Yes. We're going to have to fight our way there. They aren't just going to let us by, silly."

The birds squawked louder and louder. They flew out ahead and began circling a big rock as it came into Johnny's view. *What is it about big rocks?* he wondered. He saw a sword sticking out of it. The birds landed on the rock. Lenore and Johnny gathered in front of it.

Lenore gave Johnny a solemn look. "It's the sword of truth. You're going to need it for the journey."

"Wait. It's like the sword and the stone in the story of King Arthur, right?" Johnny stepped closer to the rock. "But what if I'm not strong enough to pull it out?" As he said this, he stopped in his tracks, startled. Lying on the ground was the skeleton of a boy the same size as him. The skeleton was wearing old dirty clothes.

Chinwag squawked. "If you can't pull it out, you die."

"Not good, Johnny," Nimoy said.

"What do you mean I die?" Johnny asked. "I just want to go home."

Lenore shrugged and held out her hand toward the skeleton. "Well, you know..."

"Little William there didn't make it," Chinwag said.

"Poooooor Willie," Nimoy added.

"But you can do it, Johnny," Mr. Buggins urged. "You're an alien."

The birds began to flap their wings. "Alien! Alien he is!" they squawked.

"I'm not an alien," Johnny replied over the birds' clatter. "I'm just a boy!"

The birds calmed back down. "Then you're dead," Chinwag said.

"Yes, he's a goner," Mr. Buggins agreed.

Johnny walked closer to get a better look at the skeleton. "He must have gotten himself dead a long time ago."

"Not really," Nimoy replied.

"We ate him," Chinwag said.

"You ate him?" Johnny replied, a tremble in his voice.

"Well, he'd been dead for a little while," Chinwag said. "We kind of picked at it."

"I like bugs," Mr. Buggins added.

"You're nasty birds," Johnny said. "You wouldn't dare eat me too, would you?"

"Food is food," Chinwag replied.

"Enough of this," Lenore said. "We must have the sword with us to find the Great Door."

Johnny looked back at Lenore. "Why can't *you* pull the sword out?"

"It's not for me to pull the sword out. It has to be you."

"Why?"

She did not answer, only stared at him. For once, the talkative birds also had nothing to say.

"But I'm just a boy and not even a very strong boy at that. I'm always picked last with every sport in gym class. I play basketball a little, but I'm not good at that either. What am I going to do with a sword anyway? I can't fight, let alone use a sword. I didn't ask for any of this!"

Lenore stood there for a few moments looking puzzled. "That sounds like it should mean something." Then she laughed it off. "I don't know what that means."

"Like I said before, he's kind of scrawny looking," Chinwag observed. "Babble, babble..."

"Maybe he should give up. He will never amount to anything anyway," Mr. Buggins said. "Rabble, rabble... you must have made a mistake in bringing him here."

Johnny's face flushed, and he started to sweat. Meanwhile, Lenore just turned back to him and stared.

"What if we went ahead without the sword?" Johnny asked.

"You wouldn't get past the stronghold, Johnny. You do want to go home, don't you?"

Johnny closed his eyes at the thought of his young life ending. He was not confident about his chances. He wondered exactly how his death would occur. *What's going to happen? Will I feel pain?* He was convinced he could not remove the sword, but another way to get out of his situation had not come to mind. He had to pull the sword out or die there next to Willie. Then he would be the meal of choice for those cackling birds. *Maybe Nimoy purposely led me here, so they could eat me.*

Johnny remembered stories in Sunday school of biblical champions overcoming great odds by the hand of God. Whether God would deliver him, he didn't know. He figured he should at least say a prayer. If God did not deliver him, Johnny would see Him soon.

He bowed his head and spoke a private prayer. Then he stepped up to the sword. His breath quickened, and his hands trembled. But as he stepped forward, he lost his footing and slipped. His hand tapped the hilt. The sword fell off the rock and clanged onto the ground.

Johnny stood there for a moment, unsure what had just happened. He looked back at Lenore.

She shrugged. "The sword wasn't in there that good to begin with. Anybody could have taken it out." She looked over at the birds. "Anyone with hands, that is."

"Bah!" Mr. Buggins cried as he spread his wings and flapped away from them.

Johnny picked up the sword. It fit perfectly in his hand. It didn't look like anything special, but it was light to the touch. He turned to Lenore. "But what happened to Willie?"

"Willie didn't try. He was convinced he couldn't do it, so he didn't." She waved her hand nonchalantly. "He just withered away while staring at the sword, never taking any action."

Johnny gazed at the sword. "What do I do with it?"

"It's a very special sword. Handle it carefully. It's a weapon of deliverance. It also can be manipulated for evil." Lenore smiled. "You've tasted the fruit of knowledge. You're of age now. You must choose between good and evil, right and wrong. You must distinguish between love and hate, courage and fear."

Mr. Buggins and Chinwag returned to Lenore, both carrying a belt and sheath. Lenore received it from them as Nimoy looked on. "Thank you," Lenore said. She handed the belt and sheath to Johnny. "For the sword. From here on, keep it with you always."

Johnny received it from her. He sheathed the sword and strung the belt around his waist. Everything fit perfectly. Even though he didn't know how to use it, strapping on the weapon gave him an added sense of confidence, at least more confidence than he had minutes earlier while considering his imminent death. "OK. Can you take me to the door now? I'm as ready as I'll ever be, I guess."

Lenore did not respond right away. She gazed at him with a half-smile. "Very well, Johnny. Follow me." She turned and danced down the path. Johnny followed, the birds circling overhead.

The path led past a small hillside. They ventured away from the path a few hundred feet and walked right up to it. Embedded into the hillside was a wall. It was partially covered with overhanging vegetation.

"Here we go. It's right here," Lenore said. The birds settled in to watch as she moved away some of the brush and exposed a large keyhole in the wall. She looked back at Johnny. "Use the sword."

Johnny unsheathed the sword and held it out, expecting that maybe she would take it from him. She nodded toward the keyhole. "Use it as a key." With hesitation, Johnny slid the sword in the keyhole, right up to the hilt. As he did the wall began to glow with a wavering amber color. Johnny took a few steps back, then turned to see Lenore staring past him. The birds were perched behind her, silent. Her half-smirk appeared almost like an expression of insanity. It frightened Johnny, but at that point he had no choice. Her eyes darted to him. "Turn the key, Johnny," she said calmly.

Chinwag squawked.

Johnny looked at the wavering image of discolored amber in front of him. "The last time I was by an odd door, I got sucked in and ended up knocked out on the ground here in Imagatorium."

"That's the path for you to get home," Lenore said.

Johnny lowered his head. "Is there another path we can take?"

"Sure, we could go another route if we wanted to go to another home, but this is your path."

Johnny took a deep breath, then turned back toward the wall. He grabbed the sword's hilt with both hands and turned it. A hollow clank echoed as it unlocked. The vision of amber did not change much. However, he felt a whiff of cooler air from inside.

"Do we have to go inside too?" Mr. Buggins squawked.

"It's much nicer here," Chinwag said.

Lenore shot the birds a look and then approached the entrance. "You could return to the way you were when I found you. If that's what you want."

"You don't have to be mean about it," Mr. Buggins snapped.

"Rude. Simply rude, babble, babble," Chinwag replied.

"What's inside exactly?" Johnny asked.

"Seeeeecrets," Nimoy said.

Lenore rolled her eyes, then pulled the sword back out and waved it toward the others. "Come on." She handed the sword back to Johnny and then stepped inside, disappearing behind the twisting colors. Johnny and the birds followed. Once they were inside, the wall returned to its original form.

CHAPTER THREE

THE STRONGHOLD

Johnny found himself in a typical spring environment for that time of year. However, the air had a stale, musty taste to it. They were standing on hilly terrain before a dirt path that curled around to places unknown. He looked at Lenore, who was scanning the area with a frown.

"The overseer's house is just down that road." She waved to the birds, who were circling around them. "Go out ahead. Report to us what you find." The birds squawked and then flew off. Lenore and Johnny started down the path.

"Will the overseer help us?" Johnny asked.

"We can borrow horses and pick up supplies for our journey," she replied. She sniffed the air and looked around. "Something doesn't feel right," she said under her breath. "I don't recognize this particular stench, but it is a stench, nonetheless. Be on guard. It must be nearby."

"What must be nearby?" Johnny asked, looking around warily.

"A stronghold."

"A stronghold? How can you recognize a stronghold, by its smell?"

"Yes, at first something doesn't smell right. It pollutes the atmosphere." Lenore stopped and lifted the brim of her hat. "You'll know it when you see it. A stronghold is pretty easy to spot, if one only cares to look."

They continued to where the path rounded the hill. Hearing squawking coming from above, they looked up. Nimoy descended and landed next to them, followed by Chinwag.

"Squawk, squawk! There's destruction at the overseer's house! It looks like there was a struggle!" Nimoy exclaimed.

"We spotted the beast," Chinwag squawked. "There are many shadows with him. I couldn't get close enough to tell what they were doing."

"Where is Mr. Buggins?" Johnny asked.

"Mr. Buggins is a good snooper," Nimoy said. "He ventured further for more snooping."

Lenore lifted the trail of her dress and picked up her pace. "Come on, Johnny. Let's get to the overseer's house and see."

That didn't seem like a good idea to Johnny. He felt like they should be running away from danger, not toward it, but he followed. They rounded the corner. It wasn't long before the overseer's house came into view. They slowed to assess what they were approaching. Smoke was rising from random places across the field leading up to the house. Swords and shields were scattered. The house itself was in shambles. The aroma of embers mingled with the already foul-tasting air. Horses and livestock roamed freely around the house, not venturing too far from it.

"What happened here?" Johnny asked, stuffing his nose under his shirt. "Where is everybody?"

"The air is a bit unbearable, isn't it?" Lenore said. "Come on, let's check the house."

They trotted farther along. As they approached, they saw a man amidst the destruction. He was sitting behind a pile of rubble, the top half of his armor exposed. His face was buried in his hand. Johnny thought that the man looked like Pastor Jason. However, he knew it couldn't be him in that strange place.

"It's the overseer," Lenore whispered as they approached him from the side. The man did not look up or acknowledge them. "Overseer, what happened here?" she shouted.

The man did not move, other than to speak. "I can't find my other half." He turned to them, revealing he had only half a face and body. The inside of his face was hollow and metallic, like the armor he was half wearing. "Have you seen it?"

"Oh my," Lenore said. She scratched the back of her head through her hat. "That's quite disturbing."

The man rose to approach them. From top to bottom, he was only half a man. However, he moved as if the other half were there. He walked up to Johnny and examined him closely.

Johnny stood back in awe. The half man indeed looked like Pastor Jason. Perhaps his other half was just invisible.

The man looked down at the sword sheathed to Johnny's side. "He has the sword."

Lenore reached up to the man's face and tapped the inside, creating a hollow echoing sound. "Disturbing indeed."

The man shook his head in response.

Johnny waved his hand where the missing half of the man's should have been. Nothing. The man stepped back.

"This doesn't make much sense," Johnny whispered.

"No, it doesn't," Lenore agreed.

"What happened?" Johnny asked.

"They attacked us. We were going along, like always, singing songs, presenting God's teaching, fellowshipping with one another. It happened so quickly. We must have let our guard down. I thought I smelled evil's stench, but I ignored it. I let it be. There were over seventy of us when they came."

"Who is 'they'?" Johnny asked.

"More like *what* were they?" the man said. He waved his hand toward them. "Shadows, flying shadows around two feet in length. Hundreds of them. We fought them off for a while, but eventually, they overtook us. They pulled each of us apart, as I'm now. Where they took the other halves, I don't know. The rest of us wandered around the neighboring fields bumping into each other. I came back to the house to see if I could find any answers. I barely got here because I had forgotten the way." He pointed at Johnny. "But you have the sword. I believe that means something."

Mr. Buggins fluttered down, squawking with urgency. "The beast is up the road!" He landed on the rubble. "It's a mean, nasty one too." He tilted his head toward the man. "Weird, very weird."

"Tell me more about the beast," Lenore said.

"Squawk, squawk... It's a greyish-white lizard with big white wings. We must turn back and get away from here. Turn back!"

"Trouble!" Nimoy cried.

"A whole lot of trouble," Chinwag agreed.

"Now, now birdies," Lenore said. "Johnny wants to get home. You couldn't possibly think of abandoning him now."

"Yes, we can," Chinwag said.

"It's his home, not ours," Mr. Buggins added.

"I don't want to die," Nimoy said.

"Can we still eat him afterward?" Mr. Buggins asked.

"You will not!" Johnny exclaimed. He unsheathed his sword and waved it at Mr. Buggins. "I would cut you to pieces first."

Mr. Buggins and the other birds squawked and flapped away from him. "Killer, killer!" Mr. Buggins protested.

"Killer alien, killer alien!" Nimoy said.

Johnny waved his sword. "I said I'm not an alien!"

"Be careful with that," Lenore said. "Although they do deserve it."

"So, he's a fighter," the man said, smirking. "That's good. He can help us recover."

Johnny backpedaled his zeal and sheathed his sword. "I'm only a boy. What can I do?"

"You're the boy with the sword," the overseer responded.

"He's right, you know," Lenore said. "You're much stronger than you think. You just don't realize it yet. Let's go to the field and check on the condition of the others."

The man turned to introduce himself to Johnny. "I'm Presbyteros, the overseer."

"Johnny," the boy replied, nodding.

At that moment there was a noise amidst the rubble. Presbyteros stopped to look down. Amongst the debris, curled into a fetal position, was a cement cherub. The cherub was clutching a brown leather book to his chest.

"Praise God. They didn't take it." Presbyteros tapped the cherub on the shoulder and reached out to lift him up. "You still have the book. Get up."

The cherub turned to face Presbyteros. "Ah!" he screamed. "You're half too!" His cement body trembled, and his lip quivered. He looked at the others. "But you two are in one piece."

"You're made of—"

"Such a cute little fellow," Lenore said, giggling as she cut Johnny off.

"You laugh, woman, but I'm charged as the keeper of the sacred book," Cement Baby Cherub replied.

"And so you are," Presbyteros said.

The cherub dusted off the book. Like the surrounding devastation, the book's poor condition was apparent.

"It's the holy book the overseer teaches from," Lenore said. "May I have a look?"

"Sure, you can," Presbyteros replied.

Cement Baby Cherub clutched the book and shook his head. Lenore reached for the book, but he snatched it away.

"Why is the book in such poor condition?" Johnny asked.

"We started getting away from the Book more and more until we only referred to it passingly just to make a point. The words and lessons were supposed to be living, but they became a tool of manipulation just like everything else. It was then that the stronghold came."

Johnny and Presbyteros turned back to the scuffle between Lenore and the cherub as they tugged back and forth on the book. Cement Baby Cherub again snatched it away. However, when they realized Presbyteros and

Johnny were watching them, they paused and smiled as if nothing had happened. Lenore nodded as if she was listening to Johnny and Presbyteros talk. Cement Baby Cherub smiled sweetly.

As soon as Presbyteros turned back and continued to tell Johnny what happened, Lenore and Cement Baby Cherub renewed their struggle.

"We were not able to fight it and its shadows. In fact, most didn't even notice." He grimaced and shook his head. "I too was weak. Before I knew it, it was too late. I was humbled. All they do now is babble inside the field to one another. They're ineffective and useless, as am I."

"No!"

"Give me that book," a voice grunted behind them. They turned to see Lenore on the ground holding Cement Baby Cherub in a headlock. Once again, despite their position, they both paused and smiled as if nothing was happening.

"What are you doing?" Johnny asked.

Presbyteros chuckled. "Cement Baby Cherub, let Ms. Lenore see the book for a while. She won't keep it. She'll give it back."

"But, but..." Cement Baby Cherub protested.

Presbyteros narrowed his eye sternly. "Cement Baby Cherub, let her see the book."

Cement Baby Cherub pouted and huffed. "OK, here then," he said.

Lenore received it from him. When the other two weren't looking, she stuck out her tongue at Cement Baby Cherub. He responded with a raspberry.

"Babble, babble," Mr. Buggins squawked.

"Rabble, Rabble," Nimoy replied.

Chinwag squawked. The birds all flew away toward the field.

Presbyteros looked back at Johnny. "But now I have hope. You have the power of the sword with you. Maybe they will listen."

Johnny sighed. "We were just hoping you could help us with horses and supplies to get me home. We hadn't intended on getting involved with you and your flock."

Presbyteros turned his half face to the side. "This is no accident. You were placed here, so that you would get involved."

"Fellas. Let's just go to the field and see," Lenore said, book in hand. "Come on, Cement Baby Cherub, follow me. You can have the book back if you agree to open it for us if we want to see something. Deal?"

"Deal," Cement Baby Cherub replied.

Lenore handed the book back to him and skipped ahead. The cherub scampered after her, clutching the book. Presbyteros walked briskly after them.

Johnny still couldn't figure out how Presbyteros could move like a normal man when he was missing half his body. He also didn't know how a cement statue could be alive. He shook his head and followed the others. "This just doesn't make any sense," he whispered under his breath. "No sense at all."

They walked beyond Presbyteros's house through a group of trees that led to an open field. As they emerged from the trees, they saw two half men wearing the same armor as Presbyteros. They were having a heated debate. Mr. Buggins had flown ahead and was sitting on one of the men's shoulders. The man did not seem to notice or react to the bird's boldness. Mr. Buggins flew away when the others approached. The two continued their debate, ignoring them.

"No, I won't share any food with you. You're just lazy!" the first man said. "Arise, ol' sluggard. Observe the ways of the ant!"

"Just because you're in charge of something you think you're high and mighty!" the second man replied. "You think you can boss people around. I don't have to volunteer, you know. Pride comes before the fall, you rat!"

"Do everything in excellence, as unto the Lord. You're neither hot nor cold. From what I remember, the Book said He will spew you out of His mouth!" The first man scowled. "You're vomit dribble!"

"What?" the second man protested.

Presbyteros scratched his head. "Yes. I think the Book says all that. Well, sort of, without the vomit dribble part."

Lenore called out to the cherub to open the book. It illuminated and levitated before her. Relevant words lifted in glowing fashion from the pages. "Hmmm... yes, there are words similar, although not really in context, but on the other hand..." She quickly turned the pages, nodding and then shaking her head. "I can't find any reference to dribbling vomit, but there's something in here about a dog returning to his own—"

"You're scowling eye offends me," the second man continued. "You shalt pluck it out!"

"But that will take away the only eye he has left," Presbyteros whispered in confusion.

"I don't think that's what the words mean," Lenore said. She continued to flip the pages. "No... no..."

"Well, Judas hung himself. So, go and do likewise."

"Uh-oh," Lenore said.

"Rabble, rabble..."

"I'm confused," the overseer said.

"Stop it!" Johnny shouted. "Why are you fighting with each other? I mean, you're not even complete. We need to find your other halves."

The two turned toward Johnny as if recognizing he was there for the first time. "Who says I'm not complete, little boy?" the first man said, waving his hand to the side. "I'm perfectly fine." He twisted his half body back to the second man and angrily shook his finger at him. "It's him who doesn't think right!"

"You, see?" the second man said, appealing to Presbyteros. "I'm the one who's right. It's backed up by Scripture. You should counsel him and get him delivered. But you're too busy talking to this alien boy and the disagreeable lady."

"I'm not an alien," Johnny responded.

"And I'm not disagreeable," Lenore replied. "Well, maybe I am to such nonsense as this."

The two half men turned back to each other and resumed their argument.

With a puzzled look on his face, Presbyteros looked away from them. "They both sound right, but I don't know. I can't think. He walked over and tried to turn the pages of the book. "I can't understand the words of the book. I need my other half. It's preventing me from seeing the truth." He rubbed his temple and then turned away.

Lenore closed the book and handed it back to Cement Baby Cherub. "These two are useless. Let's leave them and look for some of the others." She looked around and spotted a cluster of individuals farther out in the field and started walking toward them.

Johnny nudged Presbyteros out of his reverie, and the two followed her.

They approached three other half persons, all of them dressed the same as the others. There were two women, one of whom was a teen, and a man.

The man was an African American. He was singing to himself. When he saw them approach, he lowered his voice and hummed. Johnny recognized him as Ken, the music minister.

The teen was fidgeting with a small box. She was trying to open it, but with only one hand, it proved difficult.

The other woman stood next to her with her hand on her hip. Again, Johnny could not understand how this half woman balanced her stance. The woman did not hide her impatience with the girl, nor did she try to help her.

"Would you hurry up with that thing? We got more company now."

"What's the overseer doing with them?" the girl asked, her attention still on the box.

Ken continued to hum. Johnny eyed him carefully. "Ken?"

He stopped humming. "Kenaniah, my name is Kenaniah." He held out his palm to Presbyteros. "I'm the director of music for the overseer."

"That you are, Kenaniah," Presbyteros replied.

"The sound of our worship has been as good as it has ever been, but there doesn't seem to be anything behind it anymore. It's just pleasing to the ear. Something is missing."

"Yeah, your other ear," Lenore replied snarkily.

Kenaniah looked at Johnny and the sword he was carrying. "This is the sword? It's like the one that was inside of us. You talked about it before in the Book."

"Yes," Presbyteros replied. "I'm confused. But I know the boy can help us."

The half woman motioned to Presbyteros. "Well, we're not about to jeopardize our lives for this woman and a homesick kid. We must think of ourselves. That is a strong and dangerous beast. It's not fair for you to ask us to contend with it."

"You seem to know a lot about us and what we're seeking," Lenore said. "And you have already passed your judgment. Don't you notice that you're missing half of yourself?"

"We heard what you were up to. There's nothing wrong with us, except for her getting her faith to work right," she replied nodding to the girl. "Will you open it already?"

"I can't seem to—"

"Here let me help you," Lenore said.

"No, don't," the girl replied. "I must have faith."

"Yes, she must have faith," the woman said. "Don't you know the Book?"

"Yes, that's right," Kenaniah said. "She must exercise her faith."

"Sounds right," Presbyteros agreed.

"I must work through my test," the girl said.

"Yes, you're the one lacking," the woman replied. "Not me. The Book says I have never seen the righteous forsaken or His seed begging for bread. So, something is wrong with you."

Lenore asked the cherub to open the book. It lit up like before. Nobody seemed to be impressed by the book's presence. "Presbyteros, why don't you have a look?"

He leaned in at the words jumping out from the page. "Yes, there is the testing of one's faith. But we need to rely on the sword that the Maker placed inside each of us. The context of that saying is not exactly..." He looked away. "I...I cannot discern..."

"We don't need the sword inside us," the woman said. "We have the special words and common sense. Right now, we just need her to open the box."

Kenaniah pointed to Johnny and stepped toward him. "You have the sword. What do you say?"

Johnny shrugged. "All I know is that first you need to get your other halves back from whatever took it from you. You're not thinking clearly. Even I, a kid, can see that."

"Ah, what do you know?" the woman replied. "You're not even from around here."

"I can't open it," the girl muttered.

"Oh, bother," Lenore said. She snatched the box out of the girl's hand, flicked open the latch, then handed it back to her. "Now open it."

The teen hesitated but then used her thumb to open the lid. Out rolled a small seed. She held it between her thumb and index finger, the box falling to the ground.

"What is it?" Johnny asked.

"It's her seed of faith, her offering," Kenaniah said.

"It's the answer to all of my problems," the girl responded.

Lenore leaned over to look at the book. The words illuminated from the page. She looked back at the others and frowned.

"Quick, plant it now," the woman said. "Plant it now and believe."

"It's true. You cannot please the Maker without faith," Presbyteros said.

They watched as the woman scraped away dirt with three fingers, not letting go of the seed. She placed the seed firmly inside and covered it up. She stood up, glowing with expectation. For several moments, everyone was silent. Johnny looked at Lenore. She scrunched her lips and tapped her fingers together repeatedly. Lenore sighed and rolled her eyes. More time went by.

"Nothing's happening. Maybe you don't have enough faith," the woman said.

"Something's wrong with me," the girl declared with exasperation.

Lenore shot the girl a glare. "You are half!"

"No, that's not it. I must have more faith."

"I'm confused," Presbyteros muttered. "Something isn't right here."

Kenaniah stepped in front of the others. "I know. You're not worshiping enough. You need to see it beforehand and enter praise and worship first. That's it!" He began to sing a familiar song, nodding for the girl to join in, which she did. As they sang, he waved for the others to join in as well. The others did, albeit with some reluctance.

Kenaniah had a beautiful voice. Johnny couldn't help but enjoy it. Lenore danced and twirled to the imaginary sounds of music in her mind that accompanied their voices. But Johnny was still bothered by them not facing the obvious. When they finished, they shared smiles and laughter.

The girl put her hand on Kenaniah's shoulder. "That was wonderful. Thank you, Kenaniah."

"We had some church!" Kenaniah replied.

After a while, they calmed down from the temporary bliss. The woman gestured to the ground. "Still nothing. Maybe you need to plant more seeds."

"You know, maybe you didn't direct the seed correctly," Kenaniah said. "To get what you want, you need to specifically claim what your seed is for to get what you want. After all, how is the Maker going to know what you need?"

"I will, I will!" the girl exclaimed. She bowed her head and whispered a prayer. "I believe, I believe."

"You don't expect the seed to grow right now, do you?" Johnny asked, feeling frustrated. "That's not how it works."

"Shhh," the woman said.

Johnny turned back to Lenore. "There must be someone here who can help us. I'll never get home at this rate." Seeing another cluster of half people, he pointed at them. The birds had flown over toward them. "Over there. How about them?"

Lenore smiled. "Lead the way, Johnny, lead the way."

Johnny walked past the three waiting for the seed, shaking his head.

"Lack of faith," the woman said. "Maybe she should fast."

Lenore gave her a sarcastic glare.

Presbyteros stopped by Kenaniah. "You're the leader of music and praise. I have a feeling you should come with us."

Kenaniah shrugged. "If you say so."

"You're just wasting your time," the woman said. "And you're going to die. You can't fight that thing. You are what you are. We're all covered by the blood of Jesus no matter what we do."

Lenore shook her head. They left the woman and the teenage girl there. They walked by many other half people along the way. They were all dressed for battle, but they were engaged in discussions with one another about things that did not matter. No one appeared to be alarmed that they were half persons.

They reached the cluster of half people that Johnny had pointed to. Three men were arguing about the state of affairs in the neighboring Floral Kingdom.

Meanwhile, Lenore had stepped back within earshot of a circle of women who were discussing recipes. Her glance of inclusion was met with an immediate response.

A half woman looked Lenore up and down. "What are you looking at? You think you're cute because of the way you dress, don't you? You don't belong here."

"No," Lenore said in her defense. "I...I..."

"You look cute, but can you look cute and bake at the same time?" the second woman asked.

"Well, uh, no, I'm not really bakendextrous," Lenore replied.

"Oh," the first woman responded with a snobbish glare.

"Well, what do you do all day?" the other woman asked, "besides making birds talk so you won't be lonely. You know, you really should be nice to them and not lead them into danger."

"And you should learn to bake too," the first woman said.

"Who told you that I was leading the birds to danger?" Lenore asked.

"We heard it from that guy over there," the other woman replied, pointing to a man. "He heard it from an orange bird. At least I think it was an orange bird. Maybe it was pink. Yes, a pink bird."

"That's not even true," Lenore said. "It's an exaggeration. You shouldn't spread rumors about people, especially when you don't really know all the facts. It's gossip."

"Oh, I believe it by the way you're dressed," the first woman said. She looked her up and down once again.

"Gossip is such a strong word. We're not gossiping. We're sharing prayer requests. We'll pray for you."

The other woman pressed her lips together in a smirk. "Yes, we'll pray for you."

"Gosh! What's wrong with you people?" Johnny exclaimed. "Can't you see that something is wrong?"

"We're fine!" a man yelled back. "Go away and leave us alone!"

"I believe this is a crossroad," Presbyteros said. "Is there anyone here who will fight with us?"

"I respect you, Presbyteros," the man said, "but I can speak for most of us here. We have no problem fighting. We just aren't going to fight that thing. It's too personal."

"It would be too painful," a woman added. "Facing it would kill us. But you can count on me to pray for you from here. I'll stay in the field with the others. It's safe here. There's safety in numbers."

Others affirmed her words and nodded in agreement.

"How is it safe?" Johnny whispered. "They're out in the open, and that didn't protect them before."

As the others stood there affirming each other's opinion on the matter, one of the half men collapsed to the ground. The others looked down at him. After a few seconds, he faded away into nothingness. The other people turned away from him and continued their senseless discussions.

"What happened to him?" Johnny asked.

"He perished under the control of the stronghold," Presbyteros replied.

Johnny looked at Lenore, his face sad. "They don't even seem to care."

Lenore rested her hand on Johnny's shoulder. "Let's go, Johnny. We'll have to handle this with what we have, or others may perish as well."

The four of them, with Cement Baby Cherub, walked away from the field. They returned to the remains of Presbyteros's house, where they would prepare. It would be up to them. They would have to confront the stronghold themselves.

The four stepped around fallen furniture and debris inside Presbyteros's house. Lenore picked up a chair from the rubble and swiped her hand across the dust-covered seat. A dirty mist enveloped the air. Johnny covered his mouth. Lenore waved her hand. She started to sit but then thought better of it.

Presbyteros stepped over to a closet door with no handle. He called out for the cherub to stand next to him. "Well, if we're going to confront it, you two should at least have your armor. I remember that much." He pointed at the door. "Hold the book up."

The cherub held the book up. Again, it levitated from his grip, and words floated from the page, then flashed through the door. A moment later, the door unlatched itself. Presbyteros pulled the door open. Mounted neatly inside were two sets of armor, the same kind that everyone else was wearing. One set was Johnny's size, and the other looked like a perfect fit for Lenore. Presbyteros held out his hand and bowed. "Johnny, Ms. Lenore," he said, "your armor."

Lenore laughed, then clapped quietly. "Oh goodie, Johnny, this is going to be so adventurous."

Johnny rolled his eyes. Returning home seemed like it was becoming increasingly far-fetched. They walked inside to take a closer look.

The armor shone brightly. "Go ahead and try it on, Johnny," Lenore said. "You can change first." She stepped back out. "Go on." She closed the door.

Johnny sighed, then took off his outer clothing. Piece by piece, he put on the armor. It was more comfortable than he thought it would be. In fact, it was more comfortable than his regular clothing. It looked heavy, but it was actually quite light. There was a mirror inside the closet. He looked at his reflection. He looked cool. Johnny strapped the sword to his side and placed his other clothing where the armor had been. Then he stepped out of the closet with his head up and his chest out.

Lenore smiled. "My, you look great, Johnny."

"You do look great," Presbyteros said. "I'm encouraged."

Johnny smiled and nodded to Lenore. "I guess it's your turn."

She pranced past him. "Yes, yes," Lenore replied. She stepped inside, then took off her hat and glanced back out. "Now, now, no peeking, naughty, naughty."

They all shook their heads and turned away. Johnny blushed. She smiled and closed the door.

From the other side, they heard Lenore shuffling around and humming. Johnny wondered why she was not taking the matter as seriously as he felt she should. He wanted to breathe in a whiff of fresh air, but the air was still foul despite the adjustment in his senses to get used to it. He could not get the stench out of his mind. He believed he should be afraid, but maybe facing the stronghold would not be as bad as it sounded.

Lenore finally opened the door. She pranced out like a model walking on a runway, swaying her hips with each step, her hair flowing behind her. Her armor fit the slight curvature of her body. She walked past them, stopped, snapped back, then returned past them in the same fashion. She turned around smugly. "Now this is a suit!"

"You look wonderful, Ms. Lenore," Johnny said.

Lenore ran her fingers through her hair. "Well, if you're going to fight a stronghold, you might as well look good doing it."

Presbyteros walked to a nearby dresser. One of the handles was hanging off, having lost a screw. He positioned the handle to where it should be and pulled open the drawer. Inside the drawer were several swords. He handed one of them to Kenaniah. He received it with a smile as if welcoming an old friend. Presbyteros also gave him a belt and a sheath, which Kenaniah put on.

Presbyteros took out another sword and hefted it in his hand. After a few sweeping movements with his wrist, he sheathed it.

He considered the other swords, then retrieved a sleek one with a cross embedded in the handle. Presbyteros held it out toward Lenore. "Try this one."

Her eyes glistening with excitement, Lenore retrieved it with both hands. She gripped the hilt and carelessly swung it around, missing Kenaniah by inches.

"Hey, be careful with that!" Kenaniah cried.

"Oh, sorry," she said, her face reddening slightly as she sheathed the sword.

Presbyteros nodded to the others. "Well, it's getting dark. We'll get down the path under the cover of night."

"We won't be able to see," Johnny said.

"We'll have the moonlight to guide us," Presbyteros replied.

"You also have the light of the sword," Lenore said pointing to the sheath attached to Johnny's side.

He pulled the sword out and held it up. For the first time he noticed a slight illumination from the blade in the shadows of early darkness. He sheathed it, covering the light.

"Let's go," Lenore said. "The birds said the stronghold was down the path about a mile. Hopefully, we'll find the others there." They bid farewell to Cement Baby Cherub who stayed behind to look after the sacred book. The rest of them followed Presbyteros into the night. They didn't really have a plan, other than to just have faith, face the stronghold, and free the captives.

With every step, Johnny felt his heart pound within his throat. The sound of his own breath rang louder and louder in his ears. He could hear his shoes crunching the dirt beneath his feet. *What am I doing?*

Presbyteros and Kenaniah's steps on the path sounded uneven compared to the cadence of their visible halves. Meanwhile, Lenore walked on her toes with a bounce. It looked as if she would break into a dance at any moment.

Why should I trust these people? Johnny wondered. *Besides something they refer to as a stronghold, I don't even know what's out there. I don't want to face this stronghold. I can barely see the trail in front of me.* He considered unsheathing his sword, which was still glowing in its sheath, but then thought better of it. It would light up the trail, but it would also expose them.

The more they progressed, the stench in the air increased. It was at the height of Johnny's discomfort that Lenore began to hum. It was a quiet sound; however, any sound that would draw attention to them was not good. Presbyteros and Kenaniah joined in, singing the words of whatever she was humming.

"Shhhh," Johnny whispered. "Not so loud. What's wrong with you?"

In response, they lowered their voices, but they continued to sing.

Presbyteros suddenly turned and held his hand back. He pointed off the trail toward a parcel of trees in the distance. Johnny could barely make out movements in the shadows from the moonlight. Presbyteros waved for them to follow him into the brushy field. "The images are hard to make out in the dark," he said.

"We have to get closer," Kenaniah agreed.

"Any closer and I'll have to hold my breath," Lenore replied. "It's over there. Trust me."

"What about the other halves?" Johnny asked.

"They must be nearby as well. We have to inspect to see," Lenore replied.

"Maybe we can free them without it finding out we're here," Johnny said.

"That's not how it works, Johnny. When a stronghold enters your space, you must confront its foul presence by standing firm against it. Otherwise, it will think it has the right to stay and will do so for generations."

Johnny waved his hand toward Kenaniah and Presbyteros. "What about them? Look what happened to them."

"I'm afraid we didn't put up much of a fight, young one," Presbyteros replied. "But even now I can sense the presence of my other half rising in resistance."

Kenaniah nodded. "I feel it too."

"Come on. Let's creep in closer," Lenore said. She turned to Johnny. "You know how to creep, don't you?"

"Yes, I think I do."

"Sure, most boys have the talent of creeping," Kenaniah said. "But we all must be good creepers now."

Presbyteros nodded to Lenore, then unsheathed his sword. "Johnny, you better keep your sword sheathed for now because of the light." Johnny popped his wrists as he nodded back. The others unsheathed their swords, then followed Presbyteros as he crept from bush to bush, tree to tree.

They gathered behind some brush. As they did, Johnny heard hissing noises all around. He was not sure where the sounds were coming from. When he looked out, he realized they had reached their destination.

Johnny saw an enormous beast, about the size of two school buses side by side. It was light gray, at least from what he could tell in the moonlight. Its reptilian skin glistened like shiny armor. Johnny thought he could make out wings folded against its sides. He also saw its large frame rise up and down as it breathed. Next to it was a large roofless cage. Inside the cage appeared to be a gathering of people.

"There, I'm in there," Presbyteros whispered.

"How do you know?" Johnny asked.

"I just do."

Lenore focused her attention on the beast. "There you are. Nasty little booger, aren't you?"

"There's nothing little about it that I can see," Kenaniah said.

"What's all that hissing?" Johnny asked.

"Shadow imps," Lenore replied. "Putrid little shadow imps."

"Yes, I remember now," Presbyteros said. "They're the ones that pulled us apart during the attack." He looked back below to the roofless cage. "Look around the cage and over the head of the beast."

Johnny squinted his eyes to take a more focused look. "Moving shadows," he replied.

"There's no time to waste," Lenore said. "Johnny, go over there and shoo them away. Shoo, shoo, shoo them away," she repeated while flicking her wrists.

"Huh? How am I supposed to do that?"

Just then a dark hissing shadow flew over their heads. As it turned and did another pass, Kenaniah swung at it with his sword, but his weapon passed right through it. The shadow flew away from them, a hissing sound trailing behind it.

"I guess we've been found out," Presbyteros said.

"Our swords are useless against these shadows," Kenaniah noted.

"Not his sword," Lenore replied, indicating Johnny. "You fight darkness with light."

The massive beast rose and stood upright. It expanded its large wings and shook them out. Then it let out a deep snarl that roiled with antagonism. Meanwhile, the rush of hissing shadows came straight at them. Johnny froze.

Lenore hit him on the shoulder. "Quick, Johnny, pull out your sword, and tap it against ours!"

Johnny quickly unsheathed his sword, and it lit up the entire area. Presbyteros clanked his sword against Johnny's, and his sword also began to emit light. Lenore clanked hers against Johnny's while Presbyteros shared his with Kenaniah.

Seeing the light, the shadows darted away from them. Presbyteros struck one as it passed. It squealed and ignited in a dark puff of sulfur. The light from their swords made the shadow imps easy to see. After swooping upward, they began to rain down on them from above.

"Look up! They're coming down on us!" Presbyteros shouted.

They swung at the descending shadows, which were barreling down upon them. Their glowing swords sliced through the night air, causing squeals and puffs of smoke. The shadows were many.

After overcoming his initial fear, Johnny sliced away with the others. His first few swings struck their targets. Putrid smells like sulfur exploded around him. However, the next few imps struck his body with force. Although they were but shadows, he felt a physical impact just the same. He tried to knock them away with his other hand, but his hand went right through them. It was only when he hit them with the light of the sword that they were destroyed.

One after another they knocked him back until he fell to the ground, still swinging his sword. He couldn't see what was happening with the others.

One of the shadows hooked what felt like a claw into his shoulder, then another dug into him on the opposite side. He felt the sensation of his body being pulled apart, but he was able to strike one of the imps that was pulling him with his sword. It screamed and exploded into sulfuric dust.

Lenore's sword came crashing down to dispose of the other imp. "Don't split on me now, Johnny!"

Johnny scrambled to his feet. He was relieved but also very aware of how close he had come to becoming a half person like those in the cage.

As Lenore and the others gathered around him, the shadows retreated toward the beast, which spread its wings and let out a yacking roar. It flapped its heavy wings and lifted itself off the ground.

"I think you made it mad, Johnny," Lenore said.

"Me?"

"Let's attack it while we have it off guard," Presbyteros said.

"It's off guard?" Johnny asked. "It looks like it's going to attack us!"

The beast hovered over the imprisoned halves, its eyes searching back and forth as people scurried to the edges of the cage to get out of the way.

"I think it has other plans," Lenore said, looking at Presbyteros and Kenaniah.

Presbyteros nodded in agreement. "Kenaniah and I will keep it occupied while you and Johnny free the others. If it's the overseer that it wants, the overseer it will get."

"What's happening?" Johnny whispered to Lenore.

"The beast was fine when the overseer was numb like the others, but now he's a threat. The enemy's strategies are predictable. Subdue the head, and the others will scatter."

They looked toward the beast as it reached inside the cage and snatched up two of the half people in its claws. With a roar, it ascended into the air.

"It has the two who are most important to them," Lenore said, looking back into the determined faces of Presbyteros and Kenaniah. "If they fail, it doesn't matter about the others." She waved Johnny to follow her to the cage. "Come with me; our window is short."

"What about the shadows? They'll see us, won't they?"

"Come on, Johnny!" she repeated.

As Lenore and Johnny trekked down to the side of the cage, Presbyteros and Kenaniah moved toward the flying beast. It was time to face their fears and to confront the stronghold.

The light from their swords illuminated the way as Johnny and Lenore hurried toward the cage. Johnny questioned the wisdom of running toward the cage with the purpose of freeing those inside. It wasn't like the shadows couldn't see what they were doing. He was prepared to continue the fight once the shadows attacked, but how the beast was going to be handled, he did not know. He and Lenore had a role to play, and he was begrudgingly in the middle of it.

Shadows flew around them but did not attack. They darted in and out, hissing in harassment. When one got close, Johnny or Lenore swung at it, but the shadows kept their distance to avoid being struck by the light. As their harassment continued, Johnny had difficulty imagining how they were going to come out of this situation alive. Part of him wished the shadows would just attack or go away, one or the other. Their harassment was becoming mentally exhausting.

One of them got too close to Lenore. Her sword dashed it into a dissipating cloud. The smell of rotten eggs struck Johnny's face.

"Stupid little imp," Lenore snapped. "Keep moving, Johnny. We're almost there."

They felt the whoosh of swirling wind from the wings of the beast circling overhead. When they looked up, the thunder of its voice screeched down at them. It circled and then flew away, as if to indicate that he had seen them. However, it kept flying toward Presbyteros and Kenaniah. As Johnny looked up, he could have sworn he saw the other half of Presbyteros' body dangling in one of the beast's talons. He presumed the half body in its other claw belonged to Kenaniah. "It has them. It has their other halves!" Johnny cried.

"Keep moving!" Lenore yelled.

When they reached the cage, many armored half people stood aloof inside. A few of them were shackled. Some shackles were thick, and some were thin. Lenore turned back and held her sword up in case the shadows chose that moment to attack. They did not.

"How do we get inside?" Johnny asked. "Is there an entrance?"

Lenore looked around as the two of them inspected the cage further. "I don't know. I don't see one." She looked up above her. "Well, I guess they were tossed in from above. I don't see how we can climb over though."

A few of the prisoners near the bars stepped toward them, looking at the intruders with lethargic curiosity.

"Well, help us," Lenore said. "Is there an entrance?"

The prisoners did not respond; they merely continued to gaze at them.

"Oh, pumpernickel!" Lenore raised her sword and struck the bars. Her sword clanked off, to no effect. The shadows hissed even louder at the disturbance. The half people who were standing nearby did not even flinch, but Johnny caught the eye of one not too far away who instinctively jerked at his shackle in response.

Lenore turned to Johnny. "You try it."

He raised his sword and swung it at the bars. He was expecting to meet the same resistance. However, it sliced through them like butter. Johnny smiled as he proceeded to cut a large opening, the severed bars falling to the ground. When the opening was large enough, he and Lenore stepped inside.

"Come on, get out of the cage. You're free," Johnny said to the prisoners, but they just continued to stare at him and Lenore. He turned to Lenore. "They act like they don't want to be free."

Lenore pointed out to Johnny what they had not noticed before, which made their situation even more frustrating. "Look, they're still armed."

Johnny rolled his eyes at the thought that they had risked their lives and fought off foul-smelling imps for people who did not want to fight to be free. They were just like their counterparts in the field.

At that moment, his attention was drawn back to the man pulling at his shackles. He was a middle-aged African American man. As Johnny approached, the man continued to tug at the chain. "Your sword, can you handle your sword?" Johnny asked. The man didn't reply; he merely stared at Johnny. Raising his sword, Johnny swung it at the chain. It melted away. The man smiled with excitement, then looked down at the arm that had been in bondage. "The sword, can you handle your sword?" Johnny asked again.

The man looked down at the sword sheathed to his side. He pulled it out and held it up. "Yes."

Johnny and Lenore were overjoyed by the man's freedom and his willingness to join him. Johnny tapped his sword against the man's sword, and it lit up just like Johnny and Lenore's. Another prisoner approached to ignite his sword, holding it out like it was a toy. Johnny tapped his sword too. However, this person seemed more interested in marveling at the brightness of the sword than using it. This puzzled Johnny.

Lenore used her sword to strike the chains and free another. This pleased her since her sword had not worked on the bars. "Free those in shackles," she said. "Ignite the swords of those who will follow." She proceeded to do exactly that while Johnny and the African American man did likewise. In a short time, the shackles were no more. Johnny was disturbed that not everyone was enthusiastic about what they were doing, nor did they want their swords touched. They only freed those who were willing. Then they led them out of the cage. Only a third of the prisoners left the cage with them. The rest stayed back, a few of them just standing there and marveling at their illuminated swords.

Johnny was surprised that the shadows had let them free the prisoners without interference. However, as they were leaving, they all came to an abrupt halt when they heard the beast's fierce growl. They looked at the beast, who stood against the backdrop of moonlit darkness. The lights of his eyes burned with defiance. The few shadows that were still fluttering around the cage flew over to aid the beast.

Presbyteros and Kenaniah were in a battle with the stronghold. Johnny knew that the next few moments would determine their fate. He wondered if he would ever see his home again.

The beast taunted Presbyteros and Kenaniah for several moments. It plopped itself down in front of them, kicking up a whirlwind of dusty soil and gravel. The beast let out a screeching roar and fixed them with an intimidating stare, claiming ownership of them as a right. Within its grasp dangled the other halves of Presbyteros and Kenaniah. The beasts stuck its chest out and waved the other halves of their bodies at them.

As Presbyteros stood rigidly next to Kenaniah, he felt a rush of strength and clarity run through his body. They were still in danger, but he felt at peace in the midst of it. He made eye contact with his other half, who returned his gaze with a knowing look.

The beast paced back and forth, bellowing in defiance.

"Stand your ground, Kenaniah," Presbyteros urged.

"Why hasn't it just crushed our halves like the others? Wouldn't that destroy us?"

Presbyteros smiled with determination. "It can't. We have resisted its authority."

Kenaniah turned to him, matching his determined glare.

The halves within the beast's claws began to flicker. They disappeared from its grip. The beast looked around in panic. The halves reappeared and joined together with Presbyteros and Kenaniah, who were made whole. Presbyteros unsheathed the sword that was with his other half and struck it with the sword of light in his other hand. It lit up like the other one.

"Yes," Kenaniah said, doing the same.

"Let's do this."

Johnny saw the lights charging the beast. The shadow attacks started up again. However, this time there were more to fight them. Johnny looked around and saw the people around them becoming whole. This gave him more courage. "Come on!" he yelled, leading the charge against the beast.

Presbyteros's sword struck the beast. It wailed and tried to get away. The imps interfered, to their own demise. Presbyteros and Kenaniah were now joined by an army wielding light swords in the night.

The battle was short lived. The beast retreated, flying back over the cage and into the night. The imps followed.

Johnny and the others raised their swords and cheered. He looked over at Lenore with joy in his eyes. Lenore returned his gaze with a look of approval. Johnny felt the satisfaction of accomplishment. It seemed like an impossible struggle, but he had tasted victory. However, the joy that was felt was soon replaced by confusion and sadness. Some of the victors shouted at the others who had not joined them. "Come with us!" they cried out.

Those who were still only half people, who elected not to respond, started to leave the cage in an orderly fashion. They walked in the same direction after the beast and the imps. They did not react to those pleading with them that they were free from bondage. A few had already begun to grow back chains that dragged behind them as they passed.

"But you're free, Johnny pleaded with one of them. "Stay with us."

The man looked at him momentarily, then haphazardly tossed his sword on the ground. Its light faded, and he continued after the beast with the others.

Johnny and the others looked back and saw the other half people that they had left in the field earlier, now coming down the trail. They continued past those who were whole, quietly following the beast.

Johnny felt his eyes tear up. "But they're free. We fought for them, and now they're just walking away." Lenore put her arm around his shoulder and hugged him.

Presbyteros joined them. "They have chosen captivity even though others paid the price for their freedom. They love bondage more."

Johnny looked into Presbyteros's eyes, searching for hope. "Will they come back?"

"A few will. But most will not." Presbyteros held his hand out toward the many who stood with them, having been made whole. "But let's celebrate those who have been redeemed. You gave us the spark of hope, the courage to resist the stronghold." Presbyteros bowed his head to Johnny. "For this we are eternally grateful."

Lenore released him, then stepped back and bowed. "Good job, Master Johnny."

Others followed Presbyteros and Lenore's lead, taking turns thanking him for his courage.

The birds flew over and joined in. "The alien kid did it," Chinwag said to Mr. Buggins. "Maybe he is the one."

Mr. Buggins cooed.

Nimoy flew around him with glee. He squawked and then perched himself next to Johnny. "I knew you could do it! Johnny, Johnny, Johnny..." Mr. Buggins and

Chinwag joined in the praises with Nimoy, celebrating Johnny and each other.

While Johnny celebrated, he suddenly felt a strong presence observing him. Yes, there were many people around him, but this felt different. It didn't feel like an evil presence or a good one for that matter. However, he felt the presence of turmoil, a focused unrest. He could not shake it.

Lenore and Presbyteros stepped up to his side and looked up at the shadowy moonlit hill. There stood the dark silhouette of a man. His muscular shadow was so defined that Johnny couldn't tell if the man was clothed or not. Although he was at a distance, Johnny could tell that the man was staring at him. The man stood there for several moments. He did not appear to care about being noticed by those below. He made no sudden movements. He just stood there and looked down at them. After several moments, he turned and walked away, disappearing behind the hill.

"Who is he?" Johnny asked.

"No one knows," Presbyteros replied. "He's just a shadow who appears and disappears from time to time."

"Has anyone tried to talk to him?"

Presbyteros placed his arm on Johnny's shoulder. "As far as we know, no one has ever gotten close enough to do so, any way why would they? He pretty much keeps to himself."

"It just seems odd," Johnny said.

The group returned to celebrating their achievement. However, Johnny kept looking at the hill, wondering about the mysterious figure who disappeared into the darkness.

The following morning. Cement Baby Cherub took his former position at the fountain, although it needed repair. The night before, Johnny had changed back into his clothing and rested well inside a comfortable sleeping bag. When morning arrived, he was awakened by the aroma of bacon cooking over a crackling fire. He also heard Lenore and Nimoy in conversation.

"Yes, Nimoy. You can come with us to the Floral Kingdom."

"Squawk. I have cousins there, you know."

"Really? I didn't know that."

"Well, they're my fourteenth cousins on my mom's second brother's side, I think. They may not recognize me now that I'm orange."

"I like orange. It's a beautiful color, and you're such a handsome bird."

"Awwwwwwww, shucks," Nimoy replied.

"Still a stupid bird, though," Chinwag chimed in with his deep voice as he joined them.

"Smart enough to bring Johnny here," Nimoy replied. "And we won!"

"We face many battles in life," Presbyteros said. "It's important to remember the victories but also to learn from our defeats."

"She's in the Maker's hands, Presbyteros," Lenore replied softly. "One day she will come back to you; you'll see."

"Maybe so, Lenore, but I have a job to do, and that is with this flock. But if you see her..."

"I know, I know..." she responded, her voice trailing off.

Johnny focused his eyes and saw Presbyteros sitting over a fire grill. He turned the bacon over inside a large pan. Lenore was wearing a fashionable canary-yellow jumpsuit with a purple hat. She wore a matching purple belt with a large buckle that fit her slim waist. His eyes were drawn to the purple nail polish on her fingernails. Johnny marveled how she looked so fashionable and fresh, especially after going through what they had endured the night before.

"Look who's up," Lenore said.

"Good morning," Johnny replied.

"Good morning, young one," Presbyteros said. "Hope you slept well. Breakfast will be ready soon."

Kenaniah walked over with a basket of eggs and bread and sat down next to Presbyteros. "Thank you. Let me get this bacon out and get these eggs going so we can eat."

Kenaniah looked over at Johnny. "Good morning, Johnny."

"Good morning, Kenaniah," he replied sitting up.

Lenore gave Johnny a warm smile and gestured to a nearby structure. "You can freshen up over there, though you'll find the accommodation a little cruder than you're probably used to." She put one hand on her hip. "But we are roughing it, you know."

Johnny chuckled to himself.

"We'll leave after breakfast," she continued. "I know of a place where we can stay. We'll have to trek a ways inside the Floral Kingdom to get there before nightfall."

He nodded and started to make his way over to get cleaned up. Johnny walked past some workers who had already begun the process of rebuilding. They waved at

Johnny as he walked by. Johnny waved back. He entered the bathroom, which was fully intact.

He thought about the events from the previous night. They had succeeded in resisting the stronghold, but he still felt the strength of its terror. He was in a place where he had to stand up and fight back. At least that part of it felt good.

Johnny removed his clothes, lathered up with soap, and cleaned himself. It was a hurried wash-up even for a kid his age. As he washed, he felt a sting from some scratches on his face. He felt the same sensation from a scuff on his elbow. He winced at the momentary discomfort, then reached for the towel and patted his face dry. He looked into the mirror and noted that the scratches were not that bad, but he would wear them with pride. He folded the towel and set it to the side, then put on the clean clothing that had been laid out for him.

He looked back into the mirror. When he did, the mirror became misty. Thinking it strange, he went to wipe it with his hand, but when he did, it wasn't his image looking back at him. It was Lenore's. Johnny jumped back, startled. He looked around him for Lenore, but she was not there. Her image faded and was replaced by the church's picnic area. His mother, Amanda, was involved in a conversation with the others. At one point she stopped and looked around as if sensing something.

Johnny tapped the mirror. "Mom, I'm here, Mom!"

She turned back around and then returned to the conversation. The image faded, and his own image returned. "Mom!"

Johnny heard squawking coming from outside.

"Is everything alright?" Kenaniah asked.

Johnny turned and opened the door. "I'm OK, but I think I saw a vision. In the mirror I saw my mother at home."

Kenaniah nodded. "I'm sure you're eager to continue your journey. They sent me to tell you that breakfast is ready."

Johnny rubbed his eyes and looked back into the mirror again. "OK, OK, I'll be there in a minute."

Kenaniah nodded and then left.

Johnny stood there for a few moments to regain his composure. He was a little shaken, having been reminded that he was in a strange place far from home. He was more determined than ever to continue the journey to find the Great Door.

When Johnny stepped outside, he was met by the squawking of two of the birds perched nearby. He smiled. "Good morning, Chinwag. Good morning, Mr. Buggins."

"Good morning, Johnny," Mr. Buggins replied.

"Good morning," Chinwag said. "The lady said we can journey with you through the Floral Kingdom."

"Squawk... Yes, we like the Floral Kingdom," Mr. Buggins said. "There are plenty of bugs to eat there. It smells good and is so colorful."

"It sounds like a nice place," Johnny said.

"You just have to know what bugs not to eat," Mr. Buggins noted.

"Oh, I don't intend on eating bugs, so I'll be OK," Johnny said as he continued walking.

The birds flew in behind him. "Don't look the mammoths in the eye, and take care around the big beetles," Chinwag said. "Hopefully, we can also avoid trouble from the two queens and their guards."

Johnny did not know what he was talking about. "Can't be worse than what we just went through with the stronghold. But I'm open to avoid any more trouble."

They walked up to the others who had already begun eating.

"Trouble?" Lenore said as she fed a berry to Nimoy. "Are you looking for trouble?"

Nimoy happily gobbled up the berry.

"No, I want to avoid trouble if I can," Johnny said. "I just want to get home."

Presbyteros smiled. "Sometimes trouble will find you no matter what." He pointed his fork and nodded his head toward a covered plate on the chair.

"Thank you." Johnny continued to the chair and lifted the cover to expose a plate of bacon, eggs, bread, and various berries. Johnny hadn't realized how hungry he was. He hadn't eaten anything since he arrived in this strange place. He said a quick prayer and dug in.

As Johnny tasted some of the berries, Mr. Buggins flew next to him, making a clicking noise. He gave Johnny an expectant look. Johnny sighed and then tossed him a couple of berries. "Here you go, Mr. Buggins, a sweet treat."

Presbyteros turned to Lenore. "Is there anything else you think you'll need?"

"No, I think we can make it to their house by nightfall. We can take the east road from there. I haven't seen them in a long time, but they're hospitable, and they've always welcomed me. We thank you again for helping us, Presbyteros. I'll return the horses."

"It's the least we could do for you after helping purge us of the stronghold. And don't worry about the horses. We have a surplus from those who abandoned them to follow the beast. We'll pray for them to return, but they have made their own choices. Some may indeed return, but the way back for them will be difficult. But they can if they choose to. For the weapons of our warfare are not of flesh and blood but have divine power to destroy strongholds. They will have to face their own strongholds to return. It won't be easy, but it is possible."

"The air smells so much better now, doesn't it?" Kenaniah said. "I couldn't tell before, but now that it's gone everything seems refreshing. We were in its filth, but now I feel clean."

"He was such a filthy beast," Lenore said. She looked at Johnny, indicating that they were ready to go. They proceeded to make final preparations. Their supplies and rations packed, Lenore and Johnny mounted their horses. Lenore nodded to Presbyteros. "The next time I see you I'm sure everything will be rebuilt and back to normal."

Presbyteros nodded back and then walked over to Johnny. "I pray that your journey is a success and that you return home safely."

"Thank you for everything," Johnny said.

Presbyteros patted Johnny's horse. "And take care of Winds here. He's a good horse."

"Winds," Johnny replied, assuming that the horse was so named for its swiftness.

Lenore held her hand to her stomach and frowned. "His stomach sometimes gets unsettled when he's nervous," she whispered.

Winds' stomach growled, followed by another sound from his rear end. They all turned away from the permeating smell. Johnny scrunched his face. The birds squawked in protest.

"Whew!" Kenaniah said, waving his hand.

"Oh-oh!" Lenore replied. She retrieved a perfume bottle from her bag and sprayed it around, waving her hand. She smiled at Johnny's horse. "Oh, my dear Winds, it will be fine. You'll see." Lenore turned to acknowledge the birds. "You know where we're going. We'll meet you there before nightfall."

The birds flapped their wings and squawked, playfully flying around and bantering with each other before flying away down the path.

Johnny laughed inside at Lenore's classy appearance. She knew where they were going, but he did not. He had to rely on her to get home. Part of him wondered if she had led other little boys down the same path. He thought about poor ol' Willie. Willie may have been in the same spot, but he didn't get as far. Johnny bit his lip, thinking about how Willie had ended up. Although he felt good about their victory against the stronghold and the imps, what would happen next was uncertain. He looked to Lenore for reassurance. "I hope we don't have to face any more strongholds up ahead."

Lenore smiled from under the brim of her hat. "Maybe not another stronghold, Johnny, but darkness comes in many forms." She smiled and turned her horse toward the path. "For now, onward to the land of flowing beauty." She nudged the sides of her horse to move forward.

Johnny did the same. They waved their goodbyes as they ventured down the trail. Dust kicked up from their horses' hooves. They disappeared around the corner of the trail on their way to the Floral Kingdom.

Chapter Four

THE SWEET AROMA OF WAR

(The Spirit of Murder)

It was a pleasant morning. They had traveled for about an hour. A cool, gentle breeze carried a variety of fragrances. It was a small sample of what they were approaching. Although it was cool, it was not cold enough to put on a coat. The birds had flown far ahead and disappeared from view. The early chatter between Johnny and Lenore was eventually replaced by silence and the clunking of the horses' hooves on the dirt path.

Johnny was relaxed, the weight of his body conforming to the saddle as he swayed back and forth. If it wasn't for the curiosity of what was ahead of them, he could have been lulled to sleep. He wondered about Lenore and why, in the short time that he had known her, she thought nothing about putting him in harm's way. She had aided him when the imps pushed him to the ground; however, she had also led him into that situation to begin with. There she was, looking like a model as she rode her horse. She seemed carefree yet serious enough when she needed to be.

"How many times have you been to the Floral Kingdom?" he asked.

"At least a dozen times," she put her hand back into her lap. "Well, at least once, I think." She then turned back in her saddle toward Johnny. "Well, I know I've been there before because I know Gredo Graddle and Ratta Tootle. They have a lovely house, they do, a very lovely house."

"Gredo Graddle and Ratta Tootle?"

"Yes, Gredo Graddle and Ratta Tootle. They are a lovely elderly couple, simply lovely. And Ratta Tootle makes the tastiest treeperklyns you've ever had."

"Treeperklyns? I don't think I have ever had a treeperklyn before? What is it?"

Lenore held her hand out and nodded her head. "You know... a treeperklyn... It's doughy and warm. You fold it like... you know, a treeperklyn."

"OK, I think," Johnny responded, figuring that was the best answer he would get. They continued to ride in silence as the road inclined up the hill. "How long will it take us to get to the Floral Kingdom?"

"We should start seeing signs of it just over this hill. We still have to travel quite a ways, but I'm sure we'll get to the house in plenty of time before nightfall."

After a while, they approached the crest of the hill. Dozens of colors began to dominate his vision. Flowers were few where they were, but farther down the hill, the flowers almost engulfed the pathway. He thought there were way too many flowers not to have an allergy issue. However, the only impact was the dominant scents coming from them. "Wow," Johnny exclaimed .

"Beautiful, isn't it?"

"Yes, it is."

Amongst the colorful plant life were great oak trees. Their beauty was arrainged like a watchful covering of the flowers beneath them. Their branches swayed in the breeze, the green leaves dancing and giving encouragement to the rising fragrances. Johnny could almost taste the pleasant blend on the tip of his tongue.

Hearing a bird squawk overhead, Johnny looked up and pointed. It was Mr. Buggins. Lenore waved to him. Mr. Buggins descended and attempted to land on the head of Lenore's horse, but the horse shook its head to shoo him away. Mr. Buggins flapped and squawked.

Lenore patted the horse's mane. "Now, now it's OK. It's only Mr. Buggins." The horse allowed Mr. Buggins to land on its head but continued to appear annoyed. "Hello, Mr. Buggins," Lenore said. "Having a good morning?"

"Squawk. Yes, I am. I've had my fill of berries and critters."

"Where are the others?" Johnny asked.

"We split up to explore. Chinwag is by the creek, and Nimoy is with some cousins of his."

"That sounds pleasant," Lenore said. "Glad you're having a wonderful morning. Remember to be at Gredo Graddle and Ratta Tootle's house by nightfall."

Mr. Buggins turned his head and blinked. "Well, about that. Rabble, rabble... I have some bad news."

Lenore stopped her horse and set her eyes on the bird.

Johnny stopped Winds behind her. He sighed at the thought of another problem potentially interfering with him getting home. *What now?* he wondered.

"Ratta Tootle is missing."

"Missing?" Lenore asked.

"Squawk, babble, babble... And they say Gredo Graddle is in a bad way, he is, a bad way. The roses are behind it for sure."

"When was she last seen?" Lenore asked. "Where could she be?"

At that moment, they were interrupted by two six-foot flower soldiers who came out from behind an oak next to the pathway. They were daisies.

"Where could she be? That's just what we want to know," one of them responded. The two flower soldiers glared at them. White petals circled around their cakey yellow faces. They were dressed in blue uniforms with matching jackets and pants. Their shoes were polished black. They pointed what appeared to be leafy rifles at Johnny and Lenore.

Johnny started to reach for his sword but then realized the soldiers already had the advantage. One of the soldiers shot him a glance in case he didn't already get the message.

"Asteralian guards," Lenore said with a sigh, "from the family order of the Asteraceae." She shook her head. "This area is free. We're not encroaching on your land. What brings your kind away from the highlands down here? And what do you have to do with Ratta Tootle and Gredo Graddle?"

Putting the rifle down slightly, the first soldier examined her more closely. "I recognize you. Madam Lenore, isn't it?"

"That's what they call me."

"Nice colors," the second soldier replied while examining Lenore's outfit. They both put down their rifles. "The last time you were here you offended our queen by wearing a bright red outfit. You know how she feels about that color."

Lenore blushed. "Yes, I guess you could say that was a small oversight."

The first soldier stepped closer and nodded to Johnny. "So that's the kid who went after the stronghold?"

"How do you know about that?" Johnny asked. "It only happened last night."

"They sound like Rosedar sympathizers to me," the other soldier said.

Lenore rolled her eyes and huffed. "I don't know what pollen-dust gibberish you're talking about. Our concern right now is to get to Gredo Graddle's home and check on his well-being." She eyed the second soldier. "You still haven't answered my question. Why are you down here?"

The soldier snarled at her in return, but his partner held him back. "We have claimed this land because of Rosedar's aggression. Ratta Tootle was outspoken in her protest of the roses' planting themselves in the lowlands.

We believe Rosedar is behind her disappearance. There has been foul play, and Rosedar will pay for her crimes."

"And you two just happened to be on your way to Gredo Graddle's home," the other soldier said. "Suspicious, very suspicious."

"Muddle crumpets," Lenore replied. "I want to get to the bottom of what happened to Ratta Tootle as much as you do. We must go see Gredo Graddle. We're wasting time talking to you."

"Be careful, Lenore," the first soldier said. "I'm only allowing your insolence for Her Highness Daizel's sake. Don't try our patience."

"Muddle crumpets!" Lenore exclaimed, then turned to Johnny. "Isn't that muddle crumpets, Johnny?"

Johnny was confused as to why she seemed to be purposely antagonizing the flower soldiers. He did not know what a muddle crumpet was either, but he nodded agreement. "Yes, Lenore, muddle crumpets."

"I know, huh?" She put her hand on her hip and glared back at the soldiers. "I have never heard of such forwardness from a weed."

The soldiers raised their rifles at the insult. Johnny yanked his sword out of its sheath. As he did, the sword hummed and reflected in the sunlight. Seeing the sword, the two soldiers lowered their rifles again. Lenore did not flinch during this exchange but merely raised a defiant brow.

"Well, maybe we're being a little too hasty here," the first soldier said. "The situation with the roses has made us jumpy."

"Indeed," Lenore replied. "And you have no right to be here."

"Rosedar breached the truce first. We'll protect our interests. But let me make a polite request that you come with us to see Daizel. We see that you're strong. You've defeated the stronghold and would be a great asset to us as well."

"We're not going with you," Lenore replied. "We're going to see Gredo Graddle. He needs us."

The two soldiers whispered to one another. Then the first soldier turned to Lenore. "Very well. Go and console him. But if you discover proof of the roses' foul play, report it to us."

Lenore rolled her eyes. "Umm hum."

"I'll take that as a yes," the soldier replied. He turned and whistled loudly. A few seconds later, they heard a buzzing noise approaching. Two gigantic honeybees appeared, each one the size of a horse. Both bees were wearing saddles.

Winds became spooked. Johnny jerked back his reins and held his sword up, anticipating an attack. The horse shuffled in a semicircle as Johnny struggled to gain control. The horse's stomach rumbled. Then it finally calmed.

The bees landed next to the soldiers, the humming from their wings stopping momentarily. Their antennae and their compound eyes shifted toward Johnny.

"It's OK, Johnny," Lenore said. "They're the mammoths. They won't hurt you. It's the soldiers' transportation."

The soldiers tossed their rifles over their shoulders and mounted the bees. "We'll continue this conversation later." The bees rose and flew off into the morning sky.

An unpleasant odor permeated the air as Johnny sheathed his sword.

Lenore looked at Winds with empathy. The horse snorted and looked away. Lenore shook her head. "Oh, Winds..." She pulled her horse's reins and proceeded back down the path. "Make sure you stay downwind of me, Johnny."

Johnny shook his head as he followed. The incident was unusual all by itself. They had just left two angry human-sized flowers that had flown away on giant bees. Notwithstanding, he didn't understand Lenore's aggressive tone with them. "Madame Lenore, what's going on here? They could have shot us."

She laughed. "You have the sword of truth, Johnny. They wouldn't have shot me."

"You?" Johnny replied. "What about me?"

"They wouldn't have shot you either. You have the sword."

Mr. Buggins flew over to Johnny's saddle. "And you're the mighty alien from space who burned the shadows and mind melted the stronghold."

"Mind melted? What are you talking about?"

Lenore laughed.

"Well, that's what we've been telling everyone," Mr. Buggins said.

"But that's not the truth," Johnny protested. "I'm not an alien from space, and we all participated together."

"Squawk... rabble, rabble, you're alien to this place. Click, click. Maybe we did embellish things a little though." Mr. Buggins saw Lenore shaking her head. "What? It was Nimoy's idea. If they fear you, they'll leave us alone."

"It doesn't always work that way, Mr. Buggins," Lenore said. "A lie is a lie that will eventually have damaging results, especially when it's a gossummery falsitude."

Johnny rode in silence, letting Lenore's words sink in. Mr. Buggins cocked his head to the side and blinked.

"You also may have challengers wanting to prove themselves against Johnny's power."

"But I don't have any power," Johnny insisted.

"You have more power than you think," Lenore said. "But it's still wrong of them to spread such rumors."

"Rabble babble, aww, it really didn't do no harm. And it might have saved our lives. Those soldiers sure thought twice about fighting you," Mr. Buggins said. "Squawk, squawk..."

"Nevertheless, it was wrong, Mr. Buggins. You should apologize to Johnny."

"Sorry," Mr. Buggins replied after a long pause.

The two continued down the path, taking in nature's beauty, although with more urgency to reach their destination. They were mostly silent as they rode amidst the vast array of colors and shifting fragrances.

They stopped by a creek to rest for several minutes while also tending to their horses and eating some of their rations. Looking across the creek, Johnny was struck by the peculiar sight of a cluster of floating jellyfish flapping nonchalantly against the breeze. Stringy tentacles glided beneath them. Mr. Buggins persuaded Lenore to let him stay for a while as she and Johnny continued. Johnny could feel the previous day's adventure wear on him, but when he looked toward Lenore, she was as clean and flawless as ever.

The sun was beginning to set when they arrived at a cottage just off the road. It looked like a cozy little place with a pristine lawn and floral arrangements outside. The grass was green and luscious.

"That's it," Lenore said. "We have arrived."

"It seems like a nice place," Johnny observed.

"A nice place for a nice couple. Come on, Johnny. Let's hurry and see Gredo Graddle. He must be greatly bothered.

A small stable was next to the cottage. They hurriedly rode their horses inside it and then dismounted. After securing their horses near a trough, they approached the cottage. Lenore knocked. "Gredo Graddle, open up, it's Madam Lenore!"

"What's that?" an old man's voice bellowed. "Who did you say it is?"

"Lenore! Madam Lenore."

They heard shuffling inside followed by the sound of unlatching locks. "Oh my, oh my, Lenore, oh my," the man's voice said, waving. The door opened, and an old and somewhat feeble man stepped out. He was wearing gray trousers that were too short and a brown shirt that was too big. The gray hair on the sides of his head was muffed around his bald top. He had open sandals that exposed feet and toes that looked like they needed attention. His face was worn, and he looked like he had skipped a couple of shaves. His eyes were red as if he had been crying. He was hunched over.

Lenore looked at him with empathy. "Oh, my dear Gredo Graddle." She reached out to give him a hug.

Gredo Graddle shuffled forward to receive it. "Lenore, I'm glad you've come. Ratta Tootle, poor Ratta Tootle is missing, and I don't know where to find her. The Asteralians think the roses are behind it. Boo hoo hoo, boo hoo hoo. I don't know what to believe. Boo hoo hoo."

"There, there, Gredo Graddle, we'll get to the bottom of this. You'll see."

Gredo Graddle released her. He wiped his face with his hand and tried to compose himself. "Well, well, come inside," he said, finally noticing the boy.

"Gredo Graddle, this is Johnny."

Johnny nodded, not knowing how to respond to the uncomfortable situation.

"Oh, Johnny, hello. Come in, come in." Gredo Graddle shuffled over to a cluttered couch and tossed papers and other items onto the floor, then patted a cushion back into place. The entire house was a wreck. Drawers had been pulled out and scattered. Food scraps covered the table and floor. A bowl was smashed, exposing sticky oatmeal on the floor, with some smeared over a broom. "Come, sit," Gredo Graddle said.

Before she sat, Lenore picked up an overturned vase with an array of flowers scattered around it and set them to the side. Johnny sat next to her.

"I'm sorry. Since Ratta Tootle has been gone, I haven't felt much like cleaning." At the mention of his wife's name, he put his head in his hands and began to sob again. "Boo hoo hoo, boo hoo hoo."

Lenore stood to comfort him. Johnny got up with her.

Gredo Graddle held his hand up as he struggled to regain his composure. He picked up a shirt from the arm of the couch and blew his nose into it. Then he wiped his face and tossed it back onto the floor. "I don't know what happened. I woke up one morning, and she was gone. Now I'm a mess, the house is a mess, everything is a mess."

"Be strong, Gredo Graddle," Lenore said. "Did you hear anything unusual? I mean something to account for everything being thrown all over the place like this."

"Oh no, no, no, no... Everything was clean and in its right place when she disappeared. You know how meticulous Ratta Tootle is."

"Then what happened?" Johnny asked.

"I started looking for her everywhere. I looked under the cushions, in the drawers, in the stove." Gredo Graddle picked up the vase that Lenore had put to the side. He tossed the flowers away and held it close to his face. "Ratta Tootle, are you there? Ratta Tootle!"

Confused, Johnny leaned in close to Lenore. "Is Ratta Tootle a really small person, or am I missing something?"

"No, Johnny, I assure you that Ratta Tootle is as tall as I am and quite healthy."

"Then why..." Johnny stopped himself, thinking it was better not to ask about something that didn't make sense. So many things did not make sense in this place.

"How long has she been gone?" Lenore asked.

"Since yesterday morning," Gredo Graddle replied. "That was many, many moments ago."

Lenore put her hand on Gredo Graddle's shoulder and guided him to sit on the couch. "Here, Gredo Graddle, have a seat, and we'll figure this out together. But first, I'm quite sure she's not in the house."

"You don't think so?" Gredo Graddle asked, looking back and forth between Lenore and Johnny.

"No," Lenore replied, shaking her head.

Johnny nodded in agreement.

"Second, we need to clean this place up. Once Ratta Tootle returns, she won't be happy about what you did here, right?"

"No, I guess she won't," Gredo Graddle agreed, a flicker of hope in his voice.

Lenore lifted the brim of her hat, put her hand on her chin, and began patting her cheek with her finger. "Hmm..., what to do."

Johnny was tired from the long ride and was in no mood to clean up. He considered protesting, asking if they could rest first, but Lenore was deep in thought.

"No, no this won't do," Lenore said. "We need a really good cleaning lady to help us." She paced back toward the front door. Then she turned with a coy smirk that made Johnny cringe. "Cleaning ladies," she repeated. "We need cleaning ladies."

Lenore opened the front door and looked out at the horizon. Her yellow jumpsuit and purple hat contrasted against the backdrop of the setting sun. Lenore turned back toward them, keeping her head down for a few moments. Then she raised her head and looked confidently into Johnny's eyes.

Johnny's face became flushed, believing something was about to happen. Indeed, it did. Behind her appeared a whirlwind. It moved toward the house, approaching from behind her. Her clothing flapped, and her hat fluttered with the wind, and the ground beneath their feet rumbled.

Johnny heard clicking all around them. Bugs appeared, thousands upon thousands of ladybugs. They flew in on the whirlwind and came up from under the ground, creeping down from the walls.

The ladybugs were bigger than the beetles Johnny was used to, some of them up to two inches in length. They were yellow and purple, the same color as Lenore's outfit. As the bugs poured inside, Lenore did not take her eyes off Johnny. She merely smiled slyly.

Johnny and Gredo Graddle recoiled back to the couch. The ladybugs covered everything, but they did not get on Gredo Graddle or Johnny. They moved furniture around, returning utensils and other items to their places, shiny and clean. Trash and garbage were removed, and the walls were cleaned. Johnny watched in amazement as the bugs consumed the oatmeal, then arranged loaves of bread neatly in a basket.

When the ladybugs were finished, they filtered outside through the front door where Lenore stood.

As they passed, she nodded several times and thanked them for their assistance. She allowed one to crawl up on her finger. Upon closer observation, she noticed the yellow bug did not have purple spots like the others but the number twenty-four on its back. She chuckled. "A Kobe fan, I see." She let the bug go, and it scampered away with the others. "Better hurry before Mr. Buggins gets here."

Johnny didn't know what to think. He uneasy at the woman's power. She had encouraged the defeat of imps and a giant reptile. She made birds talk and had command over bugs. *If she has so much power, how come she can't just will me back home?* He began to wonder if perhaps she didn't want to.

Lenore swiped her hands together. "There, there, now that's done." She walked over to the table and pulled out a chair. "Come, come, Gredo Graddle. When's the last time you ate something?"

"Uh, I don't really know."

Johnny helped Gredo Graddle to the chair.

Lenore opened the cupboard and retrieved three plates and cups. She also took out some utensils and set them on the table, along with some dates, bananas, nuts, and butter. She and Johnny also used some of their rations to complete the supper setting.

They bowed their heads as Gredo Graddle stumbled through a blessing of the food. Then Lenore tore a piece off one of the loaves and passed it to Gredo Graddle. Johnny did the same as they filled their plates with various items. Lenore cut into the butter with her knife and spread it over her bread.

Considering that everything had just been handled by bugs, Johnny spoke what he was thinking. "This can't be sanitary." As soon as the words came out, he regretted saying them.

"The ladies are quite clean, I assure you," Lenore replied.

Gredo Graddle spread butter over his bread and then licked the butter off his knife. He held it up and looked at it. "Yes, quite clean indeed." Gredo Graddle ate heartily, as if he had not eaten in a while. He licked the butter off his fingers and then helped himself to another piece of bread.

He and Lenore ignored Johnny's hesitation. There was no attempt to explain what had just happened. Since Gredo Graddle was not concerned, and he was hungry too, Johnny decided to go with the flow.

Nimoy flew in an open window and perched on the corner of the table, eyeing them expectantly. Johnny smiled and tossed him a piece of bread. Nimoy happily devoured it.

"I don't know if he or any of those birds deserve it," Lenore said. "It's clear they've been talking about us to the flowers."

Nimoy squawked in protest.

"That's true," Johnny said. "They knew about the stronghold battle."

"Or at least what the birds chose to tell them," Lenore replied.

"What's wrong with getting some respect for our travels?" Nimoy said. "These are very dangerous plants, you know."

"Yes, and they seem extremely agitated over Ratta Tootle," Lenore replied. "I'm sure you birds have been talking about that too."

Mr. Buggins flew in and landed on the couch. "They were already talking about it. We just talked about what they were already talking about."

"Yes, I talked to both sides," Nimoy agreed. "I didn't want to discriminate between the two. They were already so angry. Squawk, I think the roses did something to Ratta Tootle."

Gredo Graddle looked at the bird with panic in his face. "Do you really think so?"

"Be quiet, you nasty birds!" Lenore scolded, shooing them away. "Don't listen to them, Gredo Graddle. They're just gossipers, and they don't know what they're talking about." Lenore changed the subject, and soon they were into another conversation.

After they had eaten and relaxed for a bit, Lenore convinced Gredo Graddle to get some sleep. Johnny helped him get into his pajamas. Johnny thought the pajamas were comical, being that they were white with polka dots and yellow happy faces all over them. But they were Gredo Graddle's favorite pajamas. He said they were a gift from Ratta Tootle. After he was tucked in, Gredo Graddle fell asleep quickly.

"Poor Gredo Graddle," Lenore said. She looked at Johnny. "Let's get some rest too. We can figure out what happened to Ratta Tootle in the morning."

Johnny sympathized with Gredo Graddle's despair, though not directly. It reminded him of when his mother, Amanda, lost her husband. Johnny was grateful that his adoptive parents had stepped in and raised him as their own. However, he didn't really get a chance to bond with his adopted father before he died. Amanda suffered greatly inside due to his death. As Johnny thought about it, he realized he hadn't been as supportive to her as he could have been, which made him want to get back home to her even more.

Lenore and Johnny went back and forth regarding who would sleep on the couch or the floor, both attempting to defer to the other. Johnny ended up on the couch, although he wasn't sure if Lenore's game of choice to decide the matter had been rigged or not. Chinwag had also arrived, and all of the birds were present.

Lenore lay quietly in her green silk pajamas as Johnny relaxed on the cushion. The house was quiet except for the steady, melodic snoring of Gredo Graddle in the other room. It took Johnny a while to get to sleep. He jerked his eyes open a few times at the thought of ladybugs crawling all over him. However, in the peace and tranquility of the night, he finally drifted off.

It was almost morning, and the sun was just beginning to rise, when Johnny was jerked out of his sleep by birds squawking. He opened his eyes and saw that Lenore had been awakened as well. They heard a distant buzzing sound that slowly increased in volume and intensity.

"More mammoths?" Johnny asked.

"Mammoths normally don't fly in packs early in the morning unless guided to do so," Lenore replied as she grabbed her sword and went to the window.

Johnny retrieved his sword and did the same. Outside, numerous shadows came out of the early sunrise backdrop. Eventually, the noise drowned out the sound of Gredo Graddle's snoring.

"Disobedient florets," Lenore said. "It seems that our Asteralian guards have returned, this time with backup."

"What do they want from us? We just got here. We don't know what happened to Ratta Tootle."

The buzzing calmed as the bees landed.

"Come on out, Lenore!" a voice shouted. "We know you and the boy are in there."

Gredo Graddle was woken by the sound. "What's that? What did he say?"

Lenore shouted toward the bedroom door, Johnny right behind her. "It's OK, Gredo Graddle. Some pesky flowers are causing a ruckus outside, that's all.

"Pesky... Well!" a female voice said. "That's not very hospitable to those who only want to protect you."

Johnny recognized the voice. It was the voice of Daisy, Pastor Jason's wife. However, in this world, he didn't know what to expect. He had figured out by now that people weren't who they really were in Imagatorium.

Gredo Graddle peeked out of the bedroom.

Lenore smiled to herself, then put away her sword. "Daizel," she said, opening the front door. "The only thing you managed to do is startle everyone in the house, Gredo Graddle included."

Approaching elegantly up the pathway to the front door was a beautiful flower woman. Her unblemished, powdery yellow face confirmed the image of who Johnny had thought her to be. She was more human looking than the thinner Asteralian guards who sat on mammoth bees behind her. She wore a powder-blue dress that complemented her light blue eyes. The dress was covered with silver and diamond sequins. Studded clamps held her white floral petals away from her face. Her gloves were green to match her slender neck and the color of her shoes.

"Lenore, Lenore, you're an amazing woman." Daizel caught a glimpse of Johnny and the glow of his sword, and she acknowledged him with a warm smile.

Lenore nodded to the guards as they walked up to stand next to Daizel. "It's you who looks like you want to start something."

Daizel turned to her guards and motioned for them to stand down. "One can never know what to expect these days with the treachery of Rosedar and the Red Guard. They want to dominate everything with their callousness. They're a heartless species, especially the Reds."

Johnny put away his sword.

"We just met with the overseer," Lenore said. "He sends his regards."

Daizel hesitated before she responded. "Of course."

"Do the roses have Ratta Tootle?" Gredo Graddle blurted.

"Well, it has to be them," Daizel replied. "Who else could it be?"

"If you don't know that for sure you shouldn't accuse," Lenore said. "By doing so you're an accuser accusing a questionable accuse."

"We were told that the roses came by and trounced Ratta Tootle's Garden." Daizel turned to her guard for affirmation, and they nodded in agreement.

"They say Ratta Tootle had a few choice words to say too!" one of the guards added.

"Is that true, Gredo Graddle?" Daizel asked.

"Well, yes, she was upset, but it was one of their armored beetles that did the damage. The rider apologized. She told Ratta Tootle the bug got its helmet twisted."

"That's an unlikely story if I ever heard one," Daizel huffed. "Why was it here in the first place?"

Johnny turned to Lenore. "A beetle that wears a helmet?"

She nodded. "Yes, Johnny. The Red Guard often ride beetles, just like the daisies ride mammoths. They wear metal helmets."

"More bugs," Johnny muttered. "Giant bugs."

Daizel turned to Johnny. "So, his name is Johnny. That's rude of you to not introduce him, Lenore. After all, I am a queen."

"Yes, so rude," Nimoy mumbled.

Lenore shot him a cold stare. Then she turned and nodded toward Daizel. "Johnny, may I present Madam Daizel, High Ruler and Queen of the Daisies, Commander and Chief of the Asteralian army."

Johnny didn't know what a proper acknowledgement was, so he merely bowed his head.

Daizel nodded in return. "Sir Johnny, champion of strongholds, what brings you to this place?"

"We're going to the valley to find the Great Door," Lenore said.

"So, I can return home," Johnny added.

"I see," Daizel replied. "That may take a while." She looked over her shoulder toward one of the mammoths. "It would be faster on one of the bees."

Johnny perked up. He looked to Lenore to say something, but she remained silent.

"I could take you there myself," Daizel continued, "but the bees won't allow just anyone to ride them. You must be of the Asteralian order to mount one. You must be one of us."

"But I'm not one of you. I'm not a flower."

Daizel chuckled, then put her arm around him and pulled him away from Lenore. "But you can become one of us, Johnny. I was just like you until I understood the depth of the roses' wickedness. I sacrificed myself to stand up for what was right. I'm a pillar for this cause. You do want to stand up for what's right, don't you?"

"Yeah, I guess so," Johnny replied. Her gentle touch and the warmth of her blue eyes provided comfort and assurance. She seemed nice, just like her alternative self-back home, but there was something he still didn't understand. "Why are the roses wicked?"

The guards huffed in exasperation. Daizel's countenance changed, and she flailed her arms and rolled her eyes. "Tell him why they're wicked!"

"They're pompous, arrogant braggarts who look down on everybody else!" one of the guards shouted.

"Yes, and they snub us due to their stature. They flaunt their floral scents," Daizel added. "They try to intimidate us with their sharpened thorns. The Yellows and the Pinks have expanded their settlements. They have enforced their will with Rosedar and her Red Guard leading the way." Daizel held her beautiful head high to project her voice. "But I have restored the daisies' pride. The daisies now have a leader to rival Rosedar. I have drawn a line in the sand. No more, I say, no more!"

Her companions shouted in agreement. Even the birds squawked in response to her tough words.

Daizel turned back to Johnny and regained her composure. "You see, Johnny," she whispered, "they are very bad." She looked at Gredo Graddle and Lenore. "And Ratta Tootle knew this."

Lenore grimaced in silence. Johnny understood from the look on her face that Lenore didn't necessarily agree with Daizel. To him, Rosedar seemed like a despicable personality, at least according to what he was being told. Furthermore, it did make sense to ride the bees, so they could reach their destination as quickly as possible. *What harm could it do? So, I would have to be accepted as one of them, some sort of honorary member.* Daizel was odd, but so was Lenore. With Lenore leading the way, they had already been exposed to danger. There was no telling what else they would run into.

Just then they heard the shuffling of many legs rumbling the ground beneath them. A strong floral scent, different from what was around them, filled the air. Johnny was taken aback by the intense aroma coming their way. The fragrance was strong, sweet, and powerful.

The Asteralian guards perked up, holding their weapons ready to their chests. Daizel turned her head and scoffed.

Against the backdrop of the rising sun, tall, red rose soldiers arrived on large beetles. The beetles were polished black. A few were metallic. Their shells appeared like impenetrable armor. Each had an iron helmet that fit around its head back to its thorax. Long antennae extended from beneath their helmets. Their six legs had saw-like ridges on them.

The red soldiers who rode them were adorned with long red blazers. Their shirts and trousers were brown. The dark green elongated stems of their necks towered majestically into the lush red floral petals on their heads. Sharp, muscular thorns protruded through the cloth. They had the same type of earthy rifles that the

Asteralian guards had strapped around their backs. They also had short swords sheathed at their sides.

The group halted behind the contingent of Asteralian guards. A few riders continued to approach the front door of Gredo Graddle's house. The group was led by one whose body was shaped like a woman. The tips of her petals were lined with solid gold. Her red dress fit snugly, pushing up her ample bosom. The dress flowed loosely below. Her shoes were gold. She held her head up with confidence and looked down at the daisies as she passed.

Despite the Asteralian guards' bold talk, they parted for them in silence. The beetles sniffed at them with their antennae as they moved out of the way. The female rose looked to the side and assessed what was in front of her. The bugs halted.

Of course, it would be her. The female rose had Ms. Rose's face and mannerisms. She was the sheriff's wife in Johnny's world, she and Daisy weren't fond of each other in his world. He could only imagine their dislike for each other in Imagatorium.

"Gredo Graddle, are these minor florets bothering you?" she asked with a condescending tone.

Johnny saw Daizel's eyes narrow as Gredo Graddle shuffled forward and bowed his head. "Madame Rosedar, your highness, the daisies came to help find my precious Ratta Tootle." At the mention of Ratta Tootle's name, he began to weep. Lenore reached out to comfort him.

Rosedar dismounted. Two of the other roses did the same. She walked up to Gredo Graddle, swaying her hips with patronizing confidence. Her red escorts scoffed at the Asteralian guards as they walked by behind her. "Dear, dear, Gredo Graddle, we have sent word throughout the Floral Kingdom. We'll do all that we can to help." She nodded at Daizel, "Despite the presence of this riffraff."

Daizel boiled with anger.

Rosedar acknowledged Lenore and then turned to Johnny. "Lenore, it's good to see you. It's been a long time. Word of your mighty exploits have reached us." She smiled at Johnny.

Mr. Buggins clicked.

"And this is the boy?"

"His name is Johnny," Lenore replied.

Johnny bowed his head and acknowledged her.

"Master Johnny," Rosedar replied with a majestic nod.

"You have a lot of nerve coming here," Daizel huffed. "So arrogant... everyone knows the roses are behind Ratta Tootle's disappearance."

"Come on, dearie, why do you spread such rumors? There's no truth to what you say." She turned to Gredo Graddle and held out her palms. "I assure you; the roses know as little as you do. You don't need any help from the weak minded. We're here now." She nodded to Lenore. "Some of those present excepted, of course."

"We're smarter than the likes of you," Daizel replied. "You try to cover your lies with boasts of superiority."

Soldiers on both sides perked up at the rising intensity.

"Oh, dearie, but we *are* superior." Rosedar puffed out her bosom and tilted her head. She turned and pointed to one of the strong roses next to her. "Just look at us."

The mighty rose responded by raising his brow and flexing his powerful, thorny bicep beneath his fitted coat.

"You should side with us, Johnny," Rosedar said. She closed her eyes and took a deep breath of her own pleasurable scent. "Smell our power."

Other roses joined in. Johnny also inhaled and was almost subdued by the fragrance.

"Impressive," Chinwag blurted.

Mr. Buggins squawked.

Daizel shot the birds a hateful glare.

Nimoy involuntarily shivered. He rocked his head up and down and shuffled his feet back and forth. "Shhhh, don't choose sides," he whispered.

"Yes, don't," Daizel snapped, glaring at Chinwag. He looked like he wanted to respond but then thought better of it.

"Babble, babble," Mr. Buggins gibbered.

Chinwag turned away from Daizel. "Rabble, scrabble," he whispered.

Lenore rolled her eyes. "This is really getting us nowhere. Such pompousness."

Gredo Graddle shuffled forward into the middle of the tension, his cheeks streaked with tears. "Everyone, stop bickering," he said, his voice trembling. "Nobody is acting like they care about what happened to Ratta Tootle. That's all I care about! If you aren't here to help, you can leave my property!"

Lenore hooked her arm around Gredo Graddle's. "He's right. Put aside your differences for a moment, and let's work together. How about if the roses search to the west up to the back hills and the daisies to the east? Johnny, the birds, and I will search the area around the house and back to the stream beyond. Let's reconvene tomorrow morning. Of course, if there's any news, we can send word immediately."

Johnny thought this was a reasonable solution to find Ratta Tootle. It also seemed to please Gredo Graddle and calm him. Johnny figured that the sooner they worked together, the sooner they could be on their way to find the Great Door. He looked to both sides to gauge their reaction. He was met by silence. No one said a word.

Rosedar looked at Johnny and finally let out a sigh. "Very well, Lenore. We'll set up camp here just west of Gredo Graddle's house and commence a strategic search."

They all looked at Daizel. She turned away with a sneer. "The daisies will hitch our camp here on the eastside. We'll search on the ground and from up above."

"We'll not have your bees flying over our camp," Rosedar replied. Her companions perked up with indignation due to the tone of her voice. "Just stay to your side."

"The same goes for you," Daizel snapped.

Lenore smiled broadly. "Great! That's settled then. Now let's leave Gredo Graddle be. You've already subjected him to much disturbance, and it's still early morning." She batted her eyes and rendered the fakest grin that Johnny had ever seen.

Rosedar gave her a lingering stare. Then she turned and smirked at Johnny. She twirled her finger for the roses to retreat as she walked away. "Remember, Johnny, the seat of power will be camped to the west." Rosedar was assisted back onto her beetle, and the roses withdrew. The great beetles crunched their way west to set up camp, their scent lingering behind.

Daizel stepped toward Johnny and spoke softly. "Why don't you join us to search to the east? That way we can teach you how to ride the mammoths."

"That would not be a good idea," Lenore replied. "It's important to maintain all appearances of neutrality while we work together to find her."

Johnny put his head down. He really did want to learn how to fly on the bees. He wondered what it would feel like. He also reasoned it was a fast way to reach their destination. But he was perplexed by Lenore's opposition.

On the other hand, he was also tempted by the lure of the roses. They were powerful and beautiful. If he could be with them, maybe he could become somebody important, a force to be reckoned with.

After some thought, Johnny concluded that the safest stance was to stick with Lenore's plan, although he still had his doubts. "Thank you for the offer, but I should stay with Lenore. We'll search as she has said."

Daizel's eye twitched. Then she smiled. "Very well, Johnny. But if you change your mind, you know where to find me." She winked, then turned around gracefully. The trail of her dress swung gently, the sequins along her hem flashing. She walked away with the Asteralian guards. On command, the garrison turned together at once and marched to the east while Daizel and the flyers mounted the bees, then flew away to set up camp.

After the two factions departed, Lenore took Gredo Graddle by the arm. "Come, Gredo Graddle, let's see what we can make for breakfast. Afterward, Johnny and I will canvas the area." He nodded and then shuffled inside with her.

Lenore lit a fire in the stove and prepared some boiled oats. Several minutes later, the pot was simmering. Lenore stirred the bubbling concoction while conversing about ordinary things as if everything was normal. Johnny thought it was an attempt to calm Gredo Graddle, which it did. She added cinnamon and honey to the mixture. Soon, the aroma coming from the pot started to replace the lingering scent from the roses' presence. None of them had much of an appetite. However, it was a way to redirect their attention away from what had just happened and from Ratta Tootle's absence. It provided a brief reprieve, but it wasn't long before they were drawn back into the reality of their situation.

"I should go with you to search," Gredo Graddle said, his voice trembling. "I just don't feel right sitting here while everybody is out looking. I have to do something."

Johnny empathized and put his hand on Gredo Graddle's back for assurance. He was very aware that Gredo Graddle was too feeble to walk or even ride on horseback. He would only slow them down. "Maybe you should stay here," Johnny said. "I'm sure we'll find out something."

"No, no I couldn't bear it. I must help."

Lenore gave the oats a final stir and then took the pot off the stove. "My dear, sweet Gredo Graddle, I understand. I love Ratta Tootle and will do whatever I can to get to the bottom of this." She smiled warmly. "You do trust me, don't you?"

"Yes, yes, of course I do, Lenore. I trust you more than anyone next to Ratta Tootle and the Creator Himself."

"Exactly. We must all trust in the Creator. I know it's hard. I sense everything will be alright." She came over and kissed him on the cheek.

"OK, Lenore. I sure hope so."

"Someone should be here in case there's a report. I'll leave Mr. Buggins and Nimoy with you. If there's a report from the flowers, it can be sent, and we all can be informed."

Gredo Graddle grimaced, then nodded begrudgingly. He and Johnny sat at the table while Lenore scooped up big spoonfuls of hot oats into ceramic bowls, then set them at the table before sitting down to join them. Gredo Graddle did not talk much, but Lenore did, even talking to herself at times. After they had eaten, Johnny assisted Lenore with the dishes.

Once they had attended to their necessities, Johnny and Lenore prepared to venture out on their search. Lenore changed into a pair of black jeans and a white blouse. Mr. Buggins and Nimoy were allowed into the house, though Lenore warned them not to say anything insensitive or stupid. Despite that direction, Johnny still questioned the wisdom of allowing the birds to stay behind, being that Mr. Buggins and Nimoy would often blurt out whatever came to mind. Nevertheless, after getting Gredo Graddle situated, leaving Mr. Buggins and Nimoy behind was what they did.

Johnny had thought they would ride their horses, but Lenore said they only had a couple of miles to cover, and it would be better to go on foot.

For several minutes they walked down a narrow path that led through an open, flowery grassland. Chinwag circled overhead, occasionally landing and ruffling his feathers. Lenore had a song in her head that Johnny did not know. She danced and hummed, periodically singing some of the nonsensical verses. "Apple corn leaves and elbow hair, western torch penguin there, treeperklyn!"

Chinwag picked up on Lenore's gaiety and squawked "treeperklyn" after her.

"How do we know what we're looking for?" Johnny asked. "I mean, I don't think we'll come across her just waiting for us to find her."

Lenore continued to dance and hum as she twirled around to face him. "I'm sure you're right, Johnny. It's much too nice outside to just stand around." She bounced back around and continued to sway her hips to the beat of her mind. "Treeperklyn..."

"Treeperklyn," Chinwag repeated.

"Why do you keep saying treeperklyn?"

Lenore stopped abruptly. "Shhhhh..." she whispered, pointing to a lizard perched on a nearby rock. Chinwag landed and waited.

To Johnny it was an ordinary lizard doing what lizards normally did, which was absolutely nothing. It was completely still but for a slight movement of its head and unevenly blinking eyelids.

Lenore crouched for a closer look. She glanced back at Johnny. "He looks suspicious," she whispered.

Johnny looked at the lizard. It blinked, oblivious to Lenore's comment or its meaning. Johnny gave it a second look to see if he had missed something. After all, one never could tell in Imagatorium. However, after a few moments, he concluded it was just a stupid lizard. Meanwhile, Lenore had not changed her posture. She remained squatting, peering at the lizard. They were frozen in a standoff as if waiting for the other to make a sudden move. "Why is it suspicious, Lenore?"

She shushed Johnny a second time.

Finally, the lizard smacked its jaws and let out a loud belch. The sound resonated like it came from a hefty adult man. It blinked again and then scurried on its way.

Lenore laughed and then stood up, satisfied. "False alarm. He wasn't suspicious at all. He just had gas."

"Maybe he ate a gassy cricket," Chinwag said.

"Maybe so." She then swerved her hand back and forth and pointed at Johnny. "Treeperklyn!"

"Didn't you say that a treeperklyn is like a donut or something?"

"Well, not quite a donut, but it's more than bread."

Johnny pretended to understand, even though he didn't. "What are you singing?"

131

"The treeperklyn song, silly. I just made it up. Don't you know it?" Lenore struck a pose by looking over her shoulder, kicking one of her legs up behind her. "But what's more important is that Ratta Tootle enjoyed making them." She put her leg back down and stepped closer to him. "Now, if we focus on treeperklyn, we may very well find her." She winked and then turned and continued to dance down the path.

Johnny scratched his head and followed. He tried to focus on a treeperklyn, but it was difficult. He had never tasted a treeperklyn, let alone seen one. He passed the belching lizard along the way. It screamed at him. Johnny was startled, but he chuckled at the surprise. "Maybe the lizard is suspicious after all."

After a time, Johnny intruded once again on Lenore's private engagement. "Besides treeperklyns, is there anything else that we should be looking for?"

"Ratta Tootle."

Again, Johnny decided to just go on with the flow of things.

They continued into the late afternoon. Their trek seemed more like a playful enjoyment of nature than a serious search for a missing person. However, Ratta Tootle was not to be found. So when evening fell, they returned to the house.

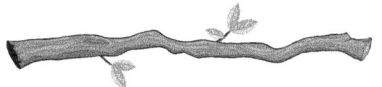

When they arrived, they found Gredo Graddle in good spirits. He, Mr. Buggins, and Nimoy were engaged in merriment, singing "Row, row, row your boat." None of them were particularly good at it. Johnny was grateful to find that the birds' pattern of irresponsible babble had not moved Gredo Graddle into further despair.

Gredo Graddle's eyes filled with hope when Lenore and Johnny arrived. Nothing had materialized from the roses or the daisies. However, Lenore assured him that they would continue the next day and that they would find her. This was enough for Gredo Graddle, who had complete trust in her.

Lenore took it upon herself once again to prepare the evening meal. Once they had their fill, Johnny helped clean up. Although they purposely did not talk much about the roses and daisies, the intensity of their dislike for each other weighed heavily on Johnny's heart. *Why can't they just forgive each other and work out their differences peacefully?*

They relaxed as much as they could until it was time for bed. Lenore changed into some shiny pink silk pajamas this time. Her matching slippers were extra fluffy. Johnny declined Gredo Graddle's night wear, choosing to sleep in his clothes.

They put Gredo Graddle to bed and gave him something to help him sleep. Then they all settled in for the night with the same unspoken worry on their minds: where was Ratta Tootle?

That night, the Asteralian guards stood erect outside of a sizable canvas tent. A flicker of light burned from within, displaying the silhouette of Daizel. Outside of the tent, floating jellyfish glowed and flapped, riding a slight breeze, their tentacles floating behind them.

The day's search had turned up no sign of Ratta Tootle. The daisies had expanded the search to include the likelihood that Ratta Tootle was dead. Now that they had settled in for the evening, Daizel was convinced that the roses were only putting on a show, especially in front of Johnny. Convincing Johnny to join the daisies could change the kingdom's power structure. It could also solidify the roses' control if the warrior-child sided with Rosedar.

A dark figure approached Daizel's tent. His steps were determined, his pace brisk. He was not one of the guards, and he was not dressed as one. He wore a slender black coat and black pants. He was a daisy of the Asteralian order. However, he lacked their beauty. Petals were missing from his head, and some that remained were brown and rotten. Abnormal indentations creased his cakey face.

As he approached the tent, one of the guards held up his hand to stop him. In response he peered at the guard with irritation. The guard gave the flower a once-over. Then he nodded to the other guard, who entered the tent to announce the flower's arrival. He came back out and held the tent flap open for the flower to enter. The flower said nothing in response as he walked inside. The guard let the flap close behind him. Then he and the other guard moved away from the tent to allow for privacy.

As the flower entered, Daizel stood to face him. He bowed before her.

"Well, what did you find?" Daizel asked.

"It's just as you suspected," the flower said, his voice raspy. "Rosedar's tent stands out from the others with its excesses. It's situated to show off its splendor rather than ensure her security."

135

"Your report pleases me. Rosedar's boastful display of arrogance will be her undoing."

"What is thy bidding?"

"You know very well what my bidding is. It's why you were called. This is going to be our best opportunity." The flower nodded his assurance. "Are you sure you can do it without being detected?"

"Our scent is weak compared to theirs. Our smell is already in the air. Our minor odor won't be unusual under the circumstances. As I have said, I can get inside undetected." The flower opened his coat to expose a dagger. "Your problem will be handled."

"Again, make it appear like it's an inside job."

"By your command."

"You will be greatly rewarded," Daizel replied.

"The price we agreed upon will be sufficient."

"Make sure it's well into the night, when she's good and asleep."

"By your command," he repeated with a bow. The flower bid his leave and exited the tent. He walked past the guards without acknowledging them and then disappeared into the night.

Rosedar lay on her cushioned bedding stuffed with goose feathers. The pillow coverings were made of silk and were fitted tightly over each one. The colors varied from red to gold and white. Rosedar's head was wrapped with a loose-fitting gold cap that covered the crown of her petals. A smaller female rose, her maiden, slept on a cot in the corner of the tent.

Rosedar had a challenging time sleeping. It seemed that every hour or so, she would wake. Her dreams merged into her thoughts when she was awake and vice versa.

The Creator had originally banished them to the hills. However, they discovered that the Creator did not interfere with their exploration of the plain. Today she had held her own in front of the contemptible Daizel. However, she envied the loyalty that some flowers had toward her. She stood out and rivaled Rosedar's space. Rosedar knew that Daizel's hatred for her helped to merge her very soul into the Asteralian order, as hers did with the roses. *I cannot allow Johnny to be swayed by Daizel's deceptive allure. Johnny's defeat of the stronghold was big, but I cannot allow an alliance with Daizel that could change what she is to me; that is, under my feet.*

Rosedar looked over at her maiden, who was snug and secure on her cot, fast asleep. Rosedar could awaken the maiden at any time and ask her to tend to her needs. However, she would not. The maiden breathed in and out in her apparent dream world of bliss.

Rosedar's mind returned to Daizel. She took a deep breath and turned over. She closed her eyes and attempted to blank her thoughts, but Daizel's cakey face sheared her consciousness. She cursed silently.

Eventually, she became groggy again, no longer able to separate the conscious from her subconscious, and she fell into a light sleep.

A sharp blade ripped through the back of the tent. It inched down, cutting an opening into the canvass. The resistance caused by its ribbed edges made the tent quiver around the cut. A gloved hand pulled back the canvas. The intruding flower wore a black head covering, his eyes peering out of two holes that were cut into it. He looked around to ascertain his surroundings inside.

He had not counted on someone else being inside the tent. However, neither his target nor the small maiden had not awakened. He was committed. He dared not face Daizel's wrath if he failed to act.

The intruder slithered inside, then stood up tall as the opening closed behind him. In one hand he gripped a towel to smother his victim's voice. In the other was the dagger. He looked around once more. Rosedar was lying to her side facing away from him. He narrowed his eyes and crept toward her. It was time to act. He held out the towel to muzzle her and raised the knife.

Before he could clamp the towel on Rosedar's face though, a piercing scream rang in his ears from the maiden behind him. Rosedar woke up and jerked around, startled. He turned back and forced her down with the towel, but she struggled against him.

The maiden jumped onto the intruder's back and tried to wrestle the dagger away, but he elbowed her in the face, causing her to jolt back.

Rosedar wriggled free from his grip to the edge of the bed. He turned back to her at the same time the guards entered the tent with their guns drawn. They shot him in the back. He collapsed onto the bed next to Rosedar.

One of the guards pulled Rosedar away. The other flung the intruder to the ground. He pounced on the flower with his knee to his back, then yanked the head covering off the lifeless body. "A daisy," he snarled.

"Are you alright?" the first guard asked Rosedar. She nodded and straightened herself up. The guards grimaced at each other in embarrassment.

Other guards also rushed in, as Rosedar's attention moved to the condition of her maiden. She demanded that they take special care of her. Then she turned upon her guards. "How could you allow this? I warned you of their evil, and now you have seen it for yourselves! Their dishonor and treachery can no longer be tolerated. Daizel will pay for this. The daisies must be eradicated. Prepare to attack!"

Guards scrambled to spread the word. Meanwhile, Rosedar stood over the deceased flower, staring down at it as anger seethed within her. She waved to the guard next to her. "Get this thing out of here." Before he could grab the body, she held up her hand. "Wait. Let's expose this plot to Lenore. She has Johnny's confidence. Let's deliver him to Gredo Graddle's house first. Afterwards, we'll rid ourselves of the daisies once and for all. Our cause is justified." Then she nodded for him to continue.

He and the other guards snatched up the daisy's body and carried it away.

Word spread quickly throughout the camp, and the roses readied for retaliation. The matter would be settled by the morning light.

Johnny was awakened by a distant commotion. He rubbed his eyes and stretched. Lenore was already awake and walking toward the window. Despite her shiny pink silk pajamas, she looked solemn. He joined her at the window.

It was the twilight of the morning dawn. The dew on the ground evaporated into light mist in the chilled air. The roses were coming. Their beetle legs pounded to a halt in front of Gredo Graddle's house, their armored bodies displaying their riders' discontent. Strapped to the back of one of the beetles was the lifeless body of a daisy dressed in black. Rosedar's contingent dismounted and approached. Red soldiers unstrapped the daisy's body and threw it onto the misty ground, then dragged it behind Rosedar.

Several daisies who had observed the roses' arrival gathered to observe the ruckus. One rode off, apparently to report what was happening.

Johnny followed Lenore to the front door. Rosedar approached with a snarl on her face. She stood aside as her soldiers tossed the daisy on the ground before them. "Look, Johnny, this is the evil of Daizel. This daisy was sent to murder me in my sleep. If it wasn't for the alertness of my maiden, he would have succeeded. My maiden is badly injured, and I pray for her welfare. My guards were able to shoot him before his dagger came down on me."

Some Asteralian soldiers rode up while Rosedar was shouting. "What are you saying?" one of the daisies yelled. They looked down at the deceased daisy on the ground.

"What have you done?" another Asteralian soldier shouted.

The roses prepared for conflict. "Don't act like you don't know, you weed," one of them said. "You tried to murder our queen. We're witnesses, and this is proof!"

"Proof? How do we know you just didn't kidnap him and kill him, just like you did to Ratta Tootle? Your species is arrogant and dishonest. From what I see, you killed one of us. This is an act of war!"

"Preposterous!" Rosedar set her eyes on Johnny. He was confused, which was evident from his face. "You can't believe such foolishness. I know if someone attacked me or not!"

Johnny didn't know whom to believe. If it was true Daizel tried to commit murder, she shouldn't be able to get away with it. Justice demanded recompense. However, maybe it was a deception by the roses. He was torn. He decided to heed Lenore's warning not to choose sides or get caught up with their bickering. However, the bickering had risen to a dangerous level. Johnny didn't want any part of it.

"Hold on, hold on," Lenore interrupted. Let's take a deep breath and step back.

Rosedar turned, boiling with rage as she eyed the daisies. "She tried to kill me. I'm not going to stand here and listen to this. If it's war you want, you'll have it. Today Daizel will pay with her own blood." Rosedar turned to leave. She nodded to the soldiers, who followed her, leaving the would-be assassin's body on the ground.

The daisies picked up their fallen comrade and carried him away.

As they left, Lenore put her arm around Johnny. He felt a pinch of sadness in his stomach. They had just been passing by, trying to get him home. They were trying to help dear old Gredo Graddle find the whereabouts of his wife. Instead they found themselves in the middle of a conflict that did not involve them and which they could not deter. Johnny understood that the spirit of resentment was always there, but now their inner turmoil had turned to violence. There was no reasoning amongst them. Both sides were prepared for war. The door to the spirit of murder had been opened, and the carnage of many would soon follow.

Gredo Graddle had not yet awakened. Lenore had allowed the birds to hunker down inside. They perched quietly and waited. Johnny slouched on the couch, the cushions sinking under the weight of his body. His blank stare fixated on the bare wall. Lenore sat upright with her legs crossed and her hands gripping the arms of the chair. Neither said a word. Everything was quiet except for the steady snoring coming from Gredo Graddle in the other room.

At first, they heard the distant popping noise of rapid gunfire. It was followed by the sound of an explosion. The humming of the bees and the crunching of beetle footsteps were intermingled with shouts of fury. Johnny hung his head. Lenore's eyes teared up.

Johnny went to the window to peek outside. What he saw was floral mayhem. Flowers fired back and forth. Some had breached close enough to engage in hand-to-hand combat. Daisies on bees zoomed in, firing sparks of light at roses riding beetles. Johnny watched as some of the daisies were hit and fell off the bees. Hoses extended from some of the beetles. They spat out chopped-up streams of liquid that scorched upon contact. An explosion ignited not too far from the front of the house. The explosion caused a beetle's front legs to crumple, throwing its red rider. The rose tried to get up but was shot several times and fell back to the ground.

The explosion woke up Gredo Graddle. "What's that? What's going on out there?"

"They're fighting, Gredo Graddle," Lenore said. "The roses and the daisies are fighting." She looked back at Johnny.

He reached for his sword. "You should see this."

"You won't need your sword, Johnny. This is a time we just stay under the covering provided for us. I've seen all of this before. It's the consequence of strife, the spirit of murder. There's no glory in it. It starts small but will only lead to death and despair. That's why they are what they are. But the Creator will soon put an end to it."

Johnny didn't know what Lenore meant, but he turned back toward the window. She went to tend to Gredo Graddle.

At that moment Johnny's attention was drawn to something that appeared out of place: a horse-drawn stagecoach moving steadily down the road toward the house. Its driver was wearing a tattered brown coat and a straw hat. He held the reins loosely as the horse maintained a steady walk.

Johnny watched floral casualties fall beside the stagecoach and an explosion erupt behind it. One of the mammoths tumbled from the sky and just missed them. Through it all, the stagecoach never changed its pace. The horse didn't startle, and the driver didn't flinch.

"Lenore, this is really odd. I think you might want to see this."

Lenore helped Gredo Graddle sit in the chair. "What is it, Johnny?"

"It's a stagecoach."

Gredo Graddle lifted his eyes and then looked away as if trying to remember something. "A stagecoach, you say?"

Lenore went to the window and joined Johnny. The stagecoach stopped in front of the house. The driver set down the reins and hopped off. A rose tackled a daisy to the ground nearby. Unfazed, the driver scratched his rear end. He then walked around the struggling flowers to the back of the stagecoach and retrieved a bag. He placed it on the ground, then stooped down to check one of the wheels. Acid from one of the beetles whizzed over his head and sizzled into the side of the road. The beetle roared past, its rider firing his weapon. The driver carried the bag to the side and opened the side door. He held out his hand to help a woman out.

Out came a plump woman in a beige dress. Her gray hair was drawn back underneath a matching sun hat. She was carrying a wicker basket. She took the driver's hand as she stepped down. She said something to the driver, who handed her the bag and then tipped his hat. The woman nodded back to him.

The driver hopped back on board the stagecoach and continued on his way. The woman turned and walked up the path toward the house. A daisy fell lifeless on the path before her. She merely stepped over him.

"By golly, it's Ratta Tootle!" Lenore said.

"Ratta Tootle!" Gredo Graddle jumped up and headed to the front door.

"Hello, hello!" Ratta Tootle shouted.

An explosion sounded off next to the house, causing it to rumble.

Lenore opened the door to allow Gredo Graddle to step out. He gave Ratta Tootle a swarming hug. "Ratta Tootle! Rattle Tootle!" Gredo Graddle cried. "I was so worried. Where have you been? Oh, Ratta Tootle..."

She stepped back for a moment to set the bag and basket down and wrapped her arms around him in return. "Ah, my dear Gredo Graddle, you forgot, didn't you? I told you that I was visiting my elder sister for a few days. I went to see Fredda Fraggle. We talked about this for weeks. Oh, ho, ho," she laughed. "All this love, you missed me?"

The violent ruckus of activity did not cease around them.

"I didn't remember and didn't know what to do. I'm thankful Ms. Lenore and Master Johnny happened to come by when they did."

"Ms. Lenore, it's been so long," Rattle Tootle said, continuing to embrace Gredo Graddle. "It's so delightful to see you again. I'm sorry to cause all of this bother." She winked. "You know his memory isn't what it used to be," she whispered. She kissed him on the forehead. "Yes, my love, I probably should have reminded you again in the morning, but you were sleeping so deeply that I didn't have the heart to wake you."

"I just woke up and realized you were gone. Yes, I do remember now. You were to leave in the morning."

"I have some treeperklyns in the basket for you, my dear. And there are plenty for everyone."

"Treeperklyns, you know how I love treeperklyns. You're too good to me, Ratta Tootle."

Lenore smiled and squinted her eyes warmly at the reunion. She hugged herself and twisted back and forth.

Johnny was relieved that Ratta Tootle was safe as well, but he thought it would be safer if they continued the reunion elsewhere. "Maybe we should take this inside," he suggested.

Lenore unfolded her arms. "Oh, Ratta Tootle, this is Johnny."

Ratta Tootle released her embrace of Gredo Graddle and acknowledged the boy. "Hello, Johnny, nice to meet you."

"We're so relieved to see you," Johnny replied. The sound of more gunfire was followed by someone yelling in anguish.

"Well, I'm sorry to cause concern, Master Johnny. Yes, let's go inside," Ratta Tootle said as she stepped in.

"And is Fredda Fraggle doing well?" Lenore asked.

"Fredda Fraggle is doing as well as can be," Ratta Tootle replied. "You know she's much older than I. She has very bad feet generally. Since birth, one foot came out bigger than the other. Not sure why that happened."

"Yes, it's very unusual," Lenore responded. "I often think about that foot. How could you not once you've seen it? But I'm glad she's well."

Johnny saw two roses crouched near the front door. "You don't have to fight anymore!" Johnny shouted. "Ratta Tootle is here safe. You can stop!"

The two roses looked his way and then turned to each other. "Kill the daisies!" one of them shouted.

"Kill the daisies," the other replied. They both ran off, firing their weapons.

Johnny assisted Ratta Tootle with her bag as the warfare continued.

Everyone went on as if what was going on outside was not happening. Johnny watched as Lenore and Ratta Tootle set the treeperklyns down and prepared coffee to go with them. They all talked and fellowshipped. Johnny was happy to finally be introduced to a treeperklyn. He took a bite, and it did not disappoint. While eating, he turned and gave a lingering stare at the front door. "How will the Creator end this, Lenore?" he asked. "When will they stop?"

Lenore and Ratta Tootle stopped talking. "We don't exactly know how He'll do it," Lenore said. "But I sense His judgment will be soon."

"They're outside of their domain, Johnny," Ratta Tootle said, setting out another treeperklyn for him. "They could have resolved their differences, but they just keep messing it up."

Just then they heard a horse neighing. Lenore looked up, recognizing the horse's cry. "Oh dear. Winds must have gotten out."

They got up and went to the door. Amid the fighting, they saw Winds running back and forth as Daizel and her multitudes moved in. Likewise, on the other side, they saw Rosedar.

"Over here, Winds!" Lenore shouted. Come this way!" Johnny waved his arms. The horse changed direction and started to head their way. However, there was an explosion right in front of him. Winds changed direction.

"I'll get him!" Johnny said.

Lenore held Johnny back and looked up at the sky. He followed her gaze. Flying toward them was a huge creature with four beige wings. It was the largest creature that Johnny had ever seen. Even the stronghold paled in size to the creature. It was taller than a seven-floor building. It was also wide and strong. Its muscles were predominant even through the loose white garment that covered its body. Its hair was like pure gold and its body like polished bronze. Carrying a sword of light, it landed hard, causing the ground to shake and dust clouds to gather under its feet. Its eyes were like burning coals.

At that moment, all the fighting and movement ceased. The creature glared at Daizel. Then, with a rush of wind caused by the turning of its head, the creature stared down Rosedar. They both recoiled. The creature bowed its head and curled in all four of its wings. When it unfurled its wings, four whirlwinds came out, increasing in size and magnitude. Johnny stood frozen in place as he stared at the spectacle.

The whirlwinds were not random but strategic, capturing the roses, daisies, bees, beetles, and weapons. Nothing that was a part of the natural landscape was affected. Rosedar attempted to pull back the beetle she was on, along with those around her, but it was as if arms of wind snatched them inside the twisting funnel. Others fled around Daizel. However, she stood defiantly with her fists balled to her sides. Then she too was snatched up.

The wind picked up in front of the house where Johnny and the others stood, but they were never threatened. It was clear that the supernatural phenomenon was not for them. After they had been scooped up by the four whirlwinds, the creature held its hand up and pointed toward the back hills. The whirlwinds circled away to where the creature pointed, with the roses, daisies, and all that they had with them.

"That was awesome!" Lenore shouted.

In the excitement, Johnny had lost sight of his horse. He looked around. "What about Winds?"

The creature turned back to face them. It unfurled one of its wings to allow Winds to clomp out from underneath. In the confusion, the creature had protected him. Winds galloped a few feet and then pranced to a stop, seeming to smile at them.

Lenore laughed and pointed both index fingers at him. "You da horse!"

Winds pranced around.

The creature swung around and spread its wings for flight. Then it lifted off the ground and flew away after the whirlwinds.

"Now that was exciting," Ratta Tootle said.

"Yes, this has been a bit much for one day, and it's still morning," Gredo Graddle replied.

"I think I want some more coffee," Ratta Tootle said. "Let's go have a spot."

"Yes," Gredo Graddle agreed. There's nothing like treeperklyns and coffee." He followed his wife inside.

"I'll go secure Winds," Johnny said.

"Thank you, Johnny. The treeperklyns will be here when you're done." Lenore gave a thumbs-up to Winds and then went inside.

Johnny was relieved that his strange adventure in the Floral Kingdom was finally over. Soon they would proceed with their journey. He guided Winds back to the stable and tended to his needs. From that moment on, Winds never again had stomach problems and was a more confident horse.

Chapter Five

THE DESCENDANTS OF LOT'S WIFE

Johnny and Lenore enjoyed their fellowship with Gredo Graddle and Ratta Tootle. They departed the next morning. Johnny had his fill of treeperklyns, and they had packed plenty more for the journey. The way Lenore told it, they would travel up the snow-peaked mountain just beyond them. Then they would go down through the valley to the other side and up beyond that, which was their destination. With the floral hills fading to their left, they began their incline trek. Lenore assured him that the climb would not be as bad as it looked from afar.

Lenore's attire seemed like a rider's outfit straight out of *Vogue* magazine. The loose-fitting beige jumpsuit appeared both comfortable and warm. She wore brown boots to match her cummerbund and a brown scarf over her head. For the life of him, Johnny could not figure out where she got her clothes from. She could not have packed them. The bag she carried was not large enough. Furthermore, nothing about the clothing looked shabby, as clothing might when unpacked after being in a bag for some time. There was not a wrinkle anywhere. She also wore large round sunglasses with brown plastic frames. Her lipstick was red. Johnny thought it was not the look of someone who planned to ride all day until nightfall.

A breeze kicked up a rush of cool air across Johnny's face. It seemed like the temperature dropped every few minutes. Winds held his neck upright and bounced his hooves in a steady rhythm. He would get up close to Lenore's horse before Johnny had to pull on the reins to slow his new inclination to lead.

As before, the birds flew around and perched themselves nearby, keeping pace with their progress. They meandered this way and that, not at all disturbed by the fact that they could fly faster than the horses could travel. As they started their ascent up the mountain trail, the birds went ahead and perched for longer periods of time. The landscape leading up the mountain was an open forest. More trees began to appear.

They stopped momentarily to rest and put on warmer coats. Afterwards, they continued their ascent. Their conversation decreased as they took in their environment. They continued well into the afternoon. The mountain vegetation was green and lush. Long grass and shrubs danced back and forth amongst massive rock formations and trees. Despite the natural foliage, the trail itself was spacious. It wove between two massive mountains, reminding Johnny of how insignificant he was in a big world. He recalled how he felt when his adopted father was ill. In the end, he could do nothing but stand by and watch the deterioration of his body. He could not ease his father's pain, and neither could his mother. He felt sad and small. The situation was so big. *Why did my real mother and father have to die? God, why did you take them from me and leave me with such emptiness? Why do you now have me with a woman who is suffering inside because of her husband's death? Death seems to follow me.*

His mind shifted to the conflict between Rosedar and Daizel. *More sadness.* Johnny's mood descended with the lowering temperature. Winds seemed to sense Johnny's thoughts and jerked his head as if to snap Johnny out of it.

"Are you alright back there?" Lenore asked.

"Yeah," Johnny replied. "I'm just thinking."

"It's better to have thoughts in your mind than to be blank, I suppose."

"Lenore, will Daizel and Rosedar ever get over their hatred of each other? Even in the face of the angel, they were still defiant."

"I know, Johnny, I know. It's often difficult to cut ties to past wrongs and move forward and forgive. I pray that one day they will."

"I mean, even many of the halfers decided to stay in bondage."

"Yes, Johnny, but be encouraged by the ones that broke away. Sometimes you need to cut your ties to the past and move forward into the hope of a bright new future without looking back. It's a choice."

He nodded in agreement, but inside Johnny still had doubts about how it applied to his own life.

"We should reach the shelters in a few hours. We'll get to a stream soon and follow it."

"There's more than one shelter?

"Yes, it's a cluster of small dwellings for travelers."

"Will there be other travelers there too?"

"There normally is, but I don't think we'll have any trouble finding a spot."

Johnny thought it would be nice to be in a warm place out of the cold, even if they had to share the space with others. However, they had not come across anyone on the trail.

A gust of wind kicked up. Johnny held the front of his coat closed and shivered. "It's getting cold," he said, his voice seeming to echo across the landscape.

"Yes, it is," Lenore replied. "If it was any colder, it would be like being in a place that was colder than it was here."

Johnny put his head down and chuckled. "Does the trail go through to where the snow is?"

"I'm not sure if we'll encounter much snow on the trail besides seeing it up around us. But it does seem that the snow on the peak is lower than normal. We'll see. We should get there and settle in before nightfall."

As they turned the bend, they saw a waterfall splashing through rocks and foaming down into a stream. Lenore smiled. "Look, Johnny, isn't it beautiful?"

He nodded. Winds perked up at the sight of the approaching stream. "I think Winds is ready for a drink."

Lenore pointed to an area that seemed like a good spot to rest. "How about stopping over there?"

"Sounds good," Johnny replied.

The birds circled overhead. "Purrrrfect spot!" Nimoy squawked against the backdrop of the rushing water. Chinwag and Mr. Buggins followed.

Lenore and Johnny dismounted and allowed the horses to graze and drink. The birds frolicked near the edge of the chilly stream. Johnny and Lenore refreshed themselves and then took in the area. He broke off a portion of a treeperklyn to snack on as he explored his surroundings. Johnny spotted a smooth rock. He picked it up and held it in his hand, then flung it into the stream. It skipped across the surface three times before it sank in the water.

"That's very good, Johnny." She picked up a rock and threw it. The rock skipped twice and then sank. Johnny grabbed another and did the same. Lenore searched around for another rock to throw. She found one that was a little flatter and smoother. It went farther than the first. Johnny got another to beat her. They spent the next few minutes skipping rocks in a friendly competition. She laughed aloud when a rock she threw did not skip at all but merely plopped into the water.

Johnny felt a bond growing between them. He couldn't remember the last time he and Amanda shared such a moment of enjoyment. Everything had always been so serious and sorrowful. With Lenore, it was the opposite. It was difficult to take her seriously even when she was being serious.

He looked up at Lenore, who was staring at him with a scrunched-up face. Her expression almost made him laugh.

"Are you OK, Johnny?"

"I was just thinking about my mother."

"Guess you miss her a lot, huh?"

"I just wish she could relax sometimes and have fun like we're having, just every once and a while."

"I'm sure it was awfully hard losing her husband. Just like how Gredo Graddle was desperate when he thought Ratta Tootle was missing."

"Yeah, I understand. But it was hard for me too. I'm just a kid and an adopted one at that. I don't have a family. I don't really have friends either."

Lenore smiled; her eyes full of sympathy. "It doesn't matter if it's only you and her now. A family is what you make of it. It's what you put into it. There will be plenty of good moments ahead. You can make a difference with that. The same goes for friends. To have friends you must be a friend. You must be friendly to potential friends. Heck, even a skoppindoddle needs friends."

"What's a skoppindoddle?" Johnny asked.

"Well, they're not very friendly, and... Oh heck, never mind," Lenore replied with a wave of her hand. "You're my friend, aren't you, Johnny?"

Johnny turned up the corner of his mouth and blushed. "Yes, Madame Lenore, I suppose I am."

"Are you my friend too?" Nimoy squawked, shaking his head after dipping it in the cool water of the stream.

"Yes, Nimoy," Johnny said. "You're my friend too."

"And me?" Mr. Buggins blurted as he circled above.

"Yes, you too, Mr. Buggins," Johnny replied.

Lenore turned to Chinwag, who was perched up next to her. "And see? Chinwag is your friend too."

Chinwag tilted his head to the side. "Uh, no," he responded.

Lenore gave Chinwag a cold glare. "You're such a naughty bird."

Johnny laughed. Lenore joined him.   It   was then that Johnny sensed a presence. He looked up and caught sight of a dark figure standing high above them on a hill. Lenore looked up to see what had caught his eye. The figure's image was distorted in the reflection of the fading sunlight. Johnny sensed it was the same mysterious man who had appeared at a distance the night they faced the stronghold. The man turned and walked away.

"Do you suppose he's following us?" Johnny asked.

"I don't know, but you probably should keep your sword close," Lenore said. "We better get going soon, so we can be there before nightfall." She pulled up the sleeve of her outfit. "But I must clean up and change out of these clothes first."

Johnny wondered again what clothes she would change into as she hadn't worn the same outfit more than once since he had arrived in Imagatorium, but instead of asking, he merely nodded and gathered his things.

As they prepared to go, Johnny saw that Lenore had changed into grey wool pants with calf-high riding boots. Her new tan coat was unzipped and matched the fresh blouse she was wearing underneath. Only a minute or so had passed from when she had said she needed to change. There was no sight of her previous clothing.

"How do you do... And what did you do with the other clothes?"

Lenore laughed and then winked at him. "They're here and there." She turned her attention to corralling her horse, who was busy grazing. She reached out, but the horse pulled back, annoyed at being disturbed. After a stern look from Lenore, the horse put its head down and submitted.

Winds, on the other hand, seemed to sense that their journey was about to continue and made his way toward Johnny. Johnny mounted Winds, and soon they were both back on the road.

The road followed the stream. As they ascended, the water rushed over rocks in the opposite direction. The temperature continued to be nippy. An hour into their journey, the trail wound away from the stream and narrowed next to the edge of the mountain. Evidence of fallen snow began to appear above and beyond them as the sun began to set.

"Are we close?"

"We're practically there. It's up and around this part of the mountain. We made perfect time."

Johnny felt relieved. He did not want to travel that path in the dark. The birds darted in and out around them. Nimoy perched on Wind's shifting saddle. Johnny looked at the sky and observed several other dark birds flying ahead. He looked down at Nimoy. "Friends of yours?"

"Babble, babble... Some are, some are not," Nimoy responded.

Areas just off the path began to show signs of occupation. Johnny observed an old, weathered wheelbarrow and an abandoned wagon. Farther on he spotted Mr. Buggins perched on a rusted ax embedded in a tree stump. The path passed under a large wooden sign. Several crows and blackbirds rested on top of it, blending into the evening twilight. Johnny didn't know how, but he could distinguish Chinwag from the other birds, although they looked alike.

The sign was chipped, its etching vaguely readable. He squinted his eyes to read the markings. "Zeboim Ranch," it said. As they continued beneath it, vapor exhaled from the horses' nostrils, and a chill swept in, making it even colder than before. A sparse blanket of white speckled the ground around them. They rode past several empty firepits. Lenore looked around, appearing to be unsure of herself. A few small log cabins were spread out farther back. They slowed their horses, the snow crunching beneath their hooves, and rode up to a semi-enclosed stable. No other horses were present, and no stable worker was in sight. In fact, they didn't see anybody. As they dismounted, Chinwag and Mr. Buggins flew inside and perched on a ledge. Nimoy flew inside too fast. He was looking back and not ahead of him, and he flew into a pile of hay. "Oh, where did that come from?" Nimoy said from inside the pile. He wobbled back out and shook himself off. Chinwag and Mr. Buggins laughed.

Meanwhile, Johnny became curious about the texture of the snow on the bottom of his scrunching shoe.

Lenore picked up a piece of ice and placed it on the tip of her tongue to taste it, then spat it out. "This isn't snow; it's salt!" They scanned the patches of what they had previously assumed was snow.

They tied the horses to the post next to the trough. Lenore pointed to a small drawer below a lantern. "These small drawers are common around here and have matches inside to light the lanterns." She opened the drawer and retrieved a box of matches. She twisted the glass opening of the lantern to expose the wick. After a few strikes, the match lit. She set fire to the wick and twisted the glass back again. She turned back to the trough. A big pump was over it to the side. Water had evaporated down, showing a chalky white ring above the water line. The horses hovered over it but did not drink. Lenore moved the pump handle up and down a few times until water began to spurt out of it.

Johnny put both hands underneath and caught some of the water. He tasted it. "Well, the pump water is OK. We just need to dump this," Johnny said, indicating the trough.

Lenore went over and began feeling beneath the trough. "From what I remember, there should be a plug on the bottom somewhere to let the water out. Ah, here it is." She gave a few twists and removed the cap. The water emptied into a drain below. She hopped back, so the water would not splatter on her boots. Johnny shook his head. He figured she would just produce more boots out of nowhere anyway.

When the trough was empty, Johnny replaced the drain plug, and then Lenore started to pump the handle to refill the trough. After a few pumps, Winds stuck his head inside and began drinking. "Come on Winds," Johnny said. "You already had your fill at the stream. You can't be that thirsty." Winds stuck his head back out and snorted before continuing.

Johnny took over for Lenore and continued to pump the water. After the trough was about half full, he slowed down due to the exertion and then stopped. The other horse joined in with Winds. Lenore and Johnny hung blankets over them that they found hanging to the side.

"Well, they'll be fine for now," Lenore said. "Let's see about the housing for the night before it gets dark. We can come back to take off the saddles and make them more comfortable later."

He nodded as they set off to find a suitable cabin for the night. Mr. Buggins and Nimoy flew with them while Chinwag was comfortable staying where he was. It was just starting to descend into twilight as they walked briskly down the trail toward the bungalows. Their breath trailed puffs of frigid air behind them. "I don't know why no other travelers are here," Lenore said. "The keeper's bungalow is right there ahead," she added, pointing.

"What's with all of this salt?" Johnny asked.

"I'm not sure, but I really want to hurry and get a place for the night."

The keeper's log cabin looked simple enough. It had one window on the side and a wooden door. Sparse patterns of salt led up to the front of the cabin and crunched beneath their feet. Above the doorway was a sign etched with black letters that read, "Home of Shemeber, Innkeeper of Zeboim. Please check in for lodging." Next to it was another sign, one that Lenore had not seen during her previous visit. It read, "We're all but the descendants of Lot's Wife." Lenore tilted her head as she pondered the words.

"What does it mean?" Johnny asked.

"I have no idea whatsoever," Lenore replied. There was no lighting coming from inside nor evidence of anyone stirring. Lenore knocked on the door. "Hello?" There was no response. She knocked again. "Shemeber, are you here?"

Johnny noticed a bell to the side and rang it. They both waited. "It looks like nobody's here," he said after a moment.

Lenore turned the doorknob. It was unlocked. The door creaked open, and she peeked inside, knocking again. "Hello?"

A quick glance revealed no sign of occupation or activity. Vaguely visible on the wall was a rack of keys numbered from one to eight. "Maybe he's tending to something," Lenore said. She snatched key number seven off the post. "I was in number seven years ago. From what I remember, it should be sufficient for us." They went out and closed the door behind them. "Come, Johnny. Let's get moving. It's getting dark. The path to number seven is just behind us, that way," she said, pointing.

They ventured down the path to two cabins that looked the same as the innkeeper. Lenore veered off to the cabin on the right. On a wooden sign to the side of the door was the number seven. They set their bags on the porch, and Lenore went to unlock the cabin, but it was already open.

They went inside. Fine salt crunched beneath their feet on the hardwood floor. The inside of the cabin was dark apart from the fading sunlight from the open doorway. Lenore pointed to the lantern on the table.

"Let me light it this time," Johnny said.

Lenore nodded for him to do so. She stepped back out onto the porch for their bags and then set them inside the cabin. She stepped back outside to give Johnny some space and to look around. She took a deep breath and watched the water vapor as she exhaled. "It's a cold night. Hopefully, we won't have an issue with the furnace."

Johnny twisted the glass of the lantern to expose the wick. It was shorter than the one in the stable. He twisted it with his fingers, then went to strike a match, but it broke off and fell to the floor. "Shoot," Johnny exclaimed.

"Are you OK in there?"

"Yeah, everything's fine."

Lenore heard squawking coming from one of the birds outside. She squinted into the failing light toward a large tree. She thought she saw something next to it but couldn't quite make it out. "Johnny, I'll be right back. I want to see what that bird is fussing about."

She stepped out and walked a short way toward the tree. As she approached it, Mr. Buggins flapped around a man who was facing away from her, concealed by shadows.

"Shemeber, is that you?" She slowed when she realized the man's stillness was due to him being a greyish-white statue, though he was wearing clothes. He was bald, and he wore a brown leather girdle and breastplate. His dark sandals were laced up his calves. An iron sword was sheathed to his side.

That's curious, Lenore thought. *That's a very odd statue*. She brushed its arm with her finger. It was coarse to the touch. *Salt?*

Mr. Buggins flapped over to the other side of the tree and landed on another frozen image. It was a salty statue of Shemeber on a horse. While she considered the horse, warm breath puffed out from its nostrils. Lenore's eyes widened, and she turned to rush back to the cabin. "Johnny!"

After a few attempts at lighting the wick, the flame took hold, sending shadows dancing around the room. Just then Johnny heard Lenore call his name. He turned to the doorway.

In the corner of the bungalow behind a partition was another statue, the frozen, salty image of a young woman. She was wearing a white toga of fine linen. She had several loose bracelets of gold on her wrists and a gold satchel around her tiny waist. Black curly locks hung from her head. Her dark lashes and eyebrows were still. Her white skin was grainy as coarse as salt.

The grit under her eyelids shifted. She opened her piercing green eyes and took a breath. Hearing voices, she slowly turned her head, her eyes narrowing.

Lenore came running up to the doorway. "Johnny, I think we need to leave. There's danger here—"

"Lenore, Lenore, don't be in such a hurry," the salt woman said as she stepped out from behind the partition.

Johnny unsheathed his sword. However, when he saw the woman, he stepped back.

She approached and looked him up and down. "Johnny boy, my little champion, such a handsome young fellow." She smirked. "Are you going to smite a defenseless woman? You know who I am, don't you, Johnny?"

"Ms. Edith?" Despite her odd appearance of salt, Johnny thought she was still quite alluring, to his embarrassment.

"You're such a smart boy, a born leader. Don't you think so, Lenore?"

"Do I know you?" Lenore asked. "I don't remember ever bumping into a salt woman before."

"No, you don't know me, but I know you. I know what you're up to. Others came before you. But to have the little champion come here himself," she snickered, "I admit I never thought of that."

Lenore's eyes opened wide. Johnny sheathed his sword and shot Lenore an inquisitive glance.

"Mankind will always repeat itself," Edith said, flaying her arms in the air. "Over and over again."

Any fear or uncertainty that Johnny had was replaced by the curiosity that somebody was there from home and acknowledged it. He thought that maybe she had also somehow fallen into that place. "Everyone I've run across from back home has been a different person in this place. Even you are different—well, your appearance is different at least."

"Yes, I guess it is," Edith responded. She held her hands to her sides. When she did, the golden bracelets she was wearing clanked against each other. "I guess I've been a little salty these days." She smirked. "Welcome to Zeboim Ranch."

"We've been on a journey to get me back home," Johnny said.

"Home?" Edith scoffed. "And what exactly awaits you there? You want to go home?" She strolled a few steps forward and gave Johnny a sultry glare. "Home is where you make it, sweetheart."

The bald salt man ran up to the doorway. Shemeber came riding up on his salt horse and dismounted outside behind him. The bald salt man had his sword drawn. Lenore stood back with her hands up as they entered. As he passed, the bald man scowled at Lenore, then turned to Edith. "Are you alright, my lady?"

She returned a coy smile. "Of course I am, Demetrius." She held out her hand to him. Demetrius sheathed his sword and then knelt and kissed it. Shemeber did the same. Then Demetrius stood up and rested his hand on the hilt of his sword. They both stood to either side of Edith, glaring at Lenore and Johnny. **"**The night has come. We live again. There's no need for alarm because of them. Our friends were just passing through. Maybe we can convince them to stay for a while." She moved in closer to Johnny and brushed his cheek with her hand, pooching out her salty lips. "Now, Johnny, let's talk some more about home."

Her closeness made Johnny feel uncomfortable, but part of him liked the attention.

Noticing the subtle flirtation, Lenore narrowed her eyes at Edith. "He's only a boy, Edith."

Demetrius stepped toward Lenore in response.

Edith laughed. "Yes, yes, he's the boy champion who one day will become a man."

Lenore pushed her shoulders back and pressed her lips together. The salt men returned Lenore's gaze, ready for any adverse movement. "Well, you shouldn't approach him like that," Lenore said, keeping her eyes on Edith.

"Tisk, tisk, so sensitive. There's no need to protect him from me." She rounded Johnny again and ogled him. "I'm quite friendly, you know."

Lenore's eye twitched.

Edith laughed in response. "Oh, Lenore, don't be such a mother hen."

"How did you get here?" Johnny asked. "How did you all come to be this way?"

"We're those who have embraced our past as defining our future. After all, we're all but the descendants of Lot's wife."

Lenore put her hand on her hip and shifted her weight, waving at Edith. "But you're salt."

"What's wrong with salt?" Demetrius shouted.

"Nothing is wrong with salt," Edith replied. "Becoming salt is not a bad thing." She twitched her hips and smiled slyly. "It's a blessing. Our eyes have been opened. We are who we are. You see, people don't really break from their past. They only pretend to. They just put on masks in front of others." She turned to Lenore and curved up the corner of her mouth. "Isn't that right, Lenore?"

Lenore gave her a cold stare.

Edith turned back to Johnny. "I'm here by choice. You see, our appearance is who we really are. It's what we choose to be, the salt of sin."

Lenore became guarded in her stance yet again. Johnny picked up on her non-verbal signals and stepped back. Demetrius and Shemeber noted their movement. The undertone of tension was becoming stressful.

"Sin? So, you embrace sin?" Lenore asked. "There's salt that is good, but that which you speak of is bad. This is bad, Johnny." She turned to plead with Shemeber. "You do know that sin is bad, right? In the end, it only leads to sorrow and death."

"I'm fine with it," Shemeber replied.

Demetrius nodded. "Good, bad, yin, yang, whatever. We do not change our nature. What we do confirms who we are."

"You can change if you choose to do so," Lenore replied. "The past does not define you."

Edith laughed dismissively. "Are you not here because of the past?"

"No, I'm here because of the future," Lenore replied.

"Is not letting go of your past a sin?" Johnny asked.

"You all seem to be uncomfortable with the term 'sin,'" Edith replied. "Let's just say there's a particular trait in us that makes us... salty and much better and happier than other people." Edith redirected the conversation. "Have you come across the dark mysterious man yet, Johnny? I'm sure he's been watching you since you arrived."

"You know of him?" Johnny asked. "We've seen the shadow of a man a couple of times watching us from a distance." He nodded at Lenore. "But why should he be watching us?"

"Watching *you*, Johnny, watching you. Lenore hasn't told you about him?"

Lenore sneered. "There's not much to tell."

"Lenore, Lenore, why do you hold such things from the boy?"

Johnny looked at Lenore.

"Don't listen to her, Johnny. She is the salt of sin. Her path is the way of destruction."

Edith laughed and threw her hands to the side, her bracelets clanking again. Then she exaggerated the rolling of her eyes. "There you go again. I'm trying not to use that word."

"He's walking his appointed path. He knows what he needs to know for his journey back home," Lenore replied. "It's his journey and his way to complete."

"Oh, but there are many paths, Lenore. There are other ways to get him where he needs to go." She nodded toward Johnny's sword. "My little champion has come this far and apparently has fought well." Her gold bracelets clanked as she waved to Demetrius. "Let's see how much he has progressed."

Before Lenore could react, Demetrius drew his sword and swung it at Johnny. Johnny's glowing sword came out with a flash and met his. Demetrius's sword swung the other way, and Johnny's sword again met it in defense. Then they stepped back from each other.

Edith let out a joyous laugh. "My, you're good, aren't you?"

Lenore froze at Johnny's sudden ability.

Johnny maintained eye contact with Demetrius, but inside he was also shocked by his own reaction. He did not understand how he had done what he did. He just knew what to do. He felt it in his spirit. His mind was a step ahead of his body and was one with his spirit. In that moment, he felt a jolt of clarity, but the feeling faded quickly.

He knew that something was not right about Edith and the salty men. He also sensed there was some level of truth that Lenore was hiding from him.

Demetrius stood upright and nodded with approval. He sheathed his sword and looked at Edith. Edith, in turn, fixed her eyes on Johnny's. "Come dine with us. Everything should be ready within the hour. We meet at the lodge's great hall for feasting... and fellowship." She smiled and flicked her wrist at Lenore, giving her a wink. "You're invited as well, Lenore."

"No, thank you," she replied. "We've had a long journey. We are just passing through and will be headed out in the morning."

Edith waited for Johnny to see if he would respond differently. He kept quiet. "Suit yourselves. We have quite a spread. Even if you choose not to stay long, you're still welcome to get what you want and replenish your food supplies."

"Thank you," Johnny said.

Edith headed toward the door. The salt men followed. Before she exited, she stopped and looked over her shoulder at Johnny. "You're most welcome, Johnny." She winked, then turned and exited the cabin. Demetrius nodded to Johnny and closed the door behind them.

There was a moment of awkward silence. Lenore fiddled around a bit before grabbing her bag from the floor and carrying it to the couch. "Well, that was different. Let's examine the rest of our lodgings to make sure there are no more salt people around." She and Johnny peeked into the other room and lit the lantern there. It revealed three bunk beds with a dresser next to each one and an attached restroom with showers. The room was plain but tidy. The only exception was the loose salt on the floor.

Johnny watched Lenore mumble to herself as she looked into the drawers and around the bunks.

"Everything looks fine. There are no cleaning ladies at this altitude, but a broom would be nice. There may be a broom in the closet out there, Johnny.

He stepped back to the closet door near the kitchenette. He opened it to find a small trash can, a broom, and a dustpan. "Here's a broom," he called out.

Lenore came out to him. "Good to know, I can get to that later. She went to the kitchen cabinets and opened one of them. Canned goods and dried noodles were inside. She raised one of the cans and read its contents, then looked back at Johnny, bit her lower lip, and shrugged.

"Edith said there was plenty of food at the lodge. Why can't we eat there or at least bring some food back here to eat?"

"Well, Johnny, they said they're fine with sin. The more we're around it, and them, the more our own morals will be corrupted by their company. We'll start to compromise. We'll lose character and become something that we are not meant to be, salty like them or something worse. We can't trust them or what they say."

"Like you want me to trust that you're really trying to help me get home?" Johnny said, unable to hide the rancor in his voice. "You lied to me."

Her eyes were full. She looked away.

"Who is the shadowy man, and why are you holding things back from me?"

Lenore moved over to the couch and sat. She turned away from him and clasped her hands in her lap. "I can't tell you," she whispered.

"You can't tell me?" Johnny asked with frustration. "I trusted you to help me get home. I believed you. You're supposed to help me get to the Great Door."

Mr. Buggins squawked at the rising of Johnny's voice. However, his squawk didn't seem to be directed at him but in his defense.

Lenore took a deep breath and turned back with sad eyes. "I didn't lie to you. I just can't tell you everything. It could interfere with your path. Sometimes if we knew what we had to face, we would never go on with the journey. We're headed in the right direction for you to go home, Johnny."

"I've been attacked by imps, threatened by a giant lizard, swarmed by bugs, and caught in the middle of a flower war. Now I'm in some godforsaken ranch where pillars of salt are alive. One just tried to kill me!"

Lenore attempted a warm smile in response. "It's your path, Johnny. You have overcome every adversity thus far. I have faith that you will continue to do so."

"This isn't a game. My mother must be worried sick. I'm sure I'm already in trouble for wandering off. I've been exposed to nothing but danger since coming here. Now some dark person is watching me, and you can't tell me why?"

"I know, Johnny. I'm asking you to have faith. I'm asking you to trust me."

"I don't know why I should," Johnny replied.

Lenore lowered her head.

Nimoy and Mr. Buggins squawked disruptively. Nimoy flapped his wings and knocked over an empty cup on the table. It bounced off the floor before rolling to a stop. Lenore and Johnny looked down at the cup, then back up to each other. That ended the conversation. She had no response, and Johnny had nothing more to say.

After a time, Johnny grabbed his coat, then he walked to the front door.

Lenore clasped her hands together as she watched him. "Where are you going?"

"I'm hungry." He opened the door.

"But Johnny..."

Nimoy flapped around her and out the door. Johnny held the door open to allow Mr. Buggins outside as well. Chinwag had flown to the porch from outside and squawked back at Lenore.

Johnny walked out and shut the door.

Johnny walked down the pathway. The salters were not hard to find. Their revelry and merriment bellowed into the frosty evening mist. The moon shone brightly, following him through the trees. When the path cleared, the moon hung above the lodge. Johnny smelled an array of smoked meat permeating the air from an opened grill. The salty patrons below were clothed in robes and sandals as if they had lived thousands of years ago in the biblical days. Several gripped mugs of wine in their hands.

A tipsy woman laughed and wrestled with a man while others urged him on. When they saw Johnny approaching, they ceased their activity and straightened up. One of them stepped into the doorway of the lodge and waved to someone inside. A moment later, Shemeber stepped out. When he made eye contact with

Johnny, he rushed back inside. The others fell silent and stepped aside as Johnny approached them. Johnny was surprised he was not afraid. In fact, he felt confident. The sound of merriment from inside the lodge settled.

"Ms. Edith invited me to join you," he said.

Those around hesitated to respond. Nimoy flapped down and perched on Johnny's shoulder. The salt man closest to Johnny eyed the orange bird and the sword to Johnny's side, then stepped back. Mr. Buggins and Chinwag flew past them. Chinwag squawked at several people around the picnic table, causing them to recoil.

Demetrius stepped out of the lodge and held his hand toward the door. "My lady, Edith, welcomes you. Come, Master Johnny. The table is set."

Johnny nodded. Nimoy flapped off his shoulder. The birds followed Johnny inside.

The lodge was filled with dozens of salt people. A few were squatting in the corner on blankets. Others stood in clusters. To the side was a table spread with delectable foods and various types of meat. A long artfully designed wooden table extended across the front with several people facing the others. In the middle sat Edith. Her chair had a high back, like a throne. Her legs were crossed, and her hands rested on the arms of the chair. Everyone fell silent when Johnny entered. It was clear to him that many were more uncomfortable with his presence than he was with theirs.

"Welcome, Johnny," Edith said, her eyes glowing. "I'm happy you were able to join us." She pointed to the food. "Enjoy whatever you want." She uncrossed her legs and leaned next to her where Shemeber sat. She tapped him to give up his seat. "You can come here and sit next to me when you get your plate."

Demetrius walked with Johnny to the table. At Demetrius's beckoning, a woman picked up a plate and looked at Johnny to indicate what he wanted. Johnny thanked her but said he wished to help himself. She looked at Edith, who nodded in response. The woman handed him the plate. Johnny recognized that whatever they had been doing before he arrived, they all had a different demeanor now as they conversed in low whispers.

After serving himself, Johnny sat down with his plate next to Edith. He bowed his head to mutter a quick prayer and bless his food. Edith eyed him silently as he did. Then Johnny bit into a piece of chicken.

Edith smiled warmly at him. "Is it to your liking?"

"Oh, yes, thank you. I never had such tasty chicken."

Edith smiled and looked at the piece of apple pie on his plate. "Try the pie. It's to die for."

Mr. Buggins squawked at her.

"Calm down, birdie. I don't mean literally." She broke off a piece from her own plate and held it up to the bird. The bird flew within inches of her, turning his head back and forth. Then he snatched the morsel and gobbled it up. He squawked with pleasure.

Johnny chuckled. He cut into the warm crust and baked apples with his fork and scooped some into his mouth. The crust melted on his tongue. The sweet apple flavor, mixed with cinnamon, made him close his eyes with pleasure.

"Told you," Edith said. She sat back in her seat while he continued to eat. "So, Lenore decided not to join us?"

"She prefers not to," Johnny replied. "She doesn't trust you."

Edith leaned forward; her eyes fixed on him. "And you trust me, Johnny?"

"Well, I'm not sure."

She sat back again and smiled. "That's a truthful response. A very mature response. It's the response of a leader, someone who is able to rule."

Johnny had no idea what she was referring to, but he received it as a cautious compliment. He decided to press in for more information. "So, who is this mysterious man, and why is he watching me? Is he trying to stop me from going home?"

"Exactly the opposite, Johnny. You may not realize it yet, but you're a threat to him. He's responsible for binding us within the borders of this ranch and to the darkness of the night. He knows you can defeat him. He knows you can set us free."

"Me? Set you free?"

"Yes, Johnny. You're adapting to this place. Your skill and knowledge are increasing. I'm sure you've noticed how you're handling the sword now. In a few days you'll be strong enough, and he knows it."

"I just want to go home."

Edith held his gaze a few moments before she responded. "Lenore knows you're getting stronger too. That's why the journey to get you home has been delayed. You were brought here to defeat him."

Things were starting to come together in his mind. There was more to him being in that strange place than what was being presented. He felt betrayed. For some reason, Lenore would not disclose the truth to him, but he didn't take what Edith was saying as the whole truth either.

Lenore had said that these people were the salt of sin. However, it didn't seem so bad the way Edith presented it. He didn't see anything outwardly evil or vile. Their skin was different, but outside of that, they seemed alright. Nevertheless, he had no desire to confront someone who wanted the same thing that he wanted, which was for him to go home as soon as possible.

"I'm not here to defeat anybody," he said. "It was a mistake for me to be here in the first place."

"Oh, Johnny, it was no mistake. You might think differently in a few days."

"I should be home in a few days."

"You know you can stay here with us for a little while until you gain your strength. We enjoy ourselves, and your inclusion would be refreshing. When you defeat him, we'll be released from the curse of daylight and the boundaries of Zeboim." She put her hand on his. Johnny looked up at her. Her hand lingered on his until he pulled it away.

"I'm not your champion, Ms. Edith. I don't want to be in Imagatorium. All I want to do is go home."

She stuck her lip out in a pout. "You don't want to help us, Johnny? I heard how you set many free from stronghold cages. I'm in a cage too. Your mercy doesn't apply to me?"

Johnny lowered his head. "Well, I hadn't thought of it that way. But my mother is probably worried about me. Don't you want to go home too?"

"What's at home, Johnny? Think about it. It's just a lot of pain and heartache. I have what I want here, absent these boundaries, and so will you. Why, you don't even have your own room at home." Then she spoke in a soothing voice of comfort. "I'm sorry, Johnny, but since your adopted father died you have only been a burden to Amanda. I sense these things."

Her words stung Johnny deeply. However, she had merely voiced something that he had already thought in his heart. Edith placed her hand on his shoulder. "Stay with me. You're important in this place. You're important to us. You can create order here." She leaned in close to his ear, her voice barely a whisper. "In time you can defeat him and then return to me. You and I can rule Imagatorium together."

An echo in Johnny's spirit felt that something was not right. However, another part of him was energized. She had presented him with an opportunity for a new life, a life where others had to look up to him. He would not be the quiet introverted kid with no father and an adopted mother who was not responsive to him. He would be somebody to be reckoned with.

The sword at Johnny's side wavered with illumination as if trying to speak. Edith glanced at the sword and then back at Johnny. "Just say the word. You can become one of us, except that, unlike us, you won't be bound inside the ranch." She held out her hand.

Johnny stared at her hand for several moments. Chinwag interrupted with a loud squawk and flapped in between them. Johnny's sword flared and hummed. Johnny was distracted by it.

"Damn birds," Edith whispered under her breath.

"Ms. Edith, I appreciate the hospitality, but I really need to leave here and go home."

Edith scoffed and waved off the birds. Then she sat back in her chair, her countenance changed.

"If he won't voluntarily join us, maybe he will by force," Demetrius whispered.

"My beam will transform him," Edith replied. "Be ready. I'll take my shot when I'm able."

Demetrius nodded slightly.

She put her hands under the table. They began to glow from within with an emerald-green color.

Out of the corner of his eye, Johnny sensed he only had a few seconds to react to whatever was about to happen. He dashed to the end of the table just as Edith pulled her hands up. Johnny ducked behind Shemeber.

Green beams of light shot from her hands and hit Shemeber in the chest. He was obliterated amongst flying salt. Johnny pulled out his sword and fell back. The impact of salt smacking his face hurt, stinging his eyes.

Just then the door flung open with a gush of wind, and Lenore entered, her sword drawn. She was wearing a black one-piece baggy pants suit with padded shoulders. The outfit was tapered around her waist. She was also wearing bright red lipstick.

"Hello, Johnny. Need a hand?"

Edith gnashed her teeth and sneered. "Lenore, you're such a pest." Then she smirked. "But I have to admit, that outfit is slamming hot!"

Lenore reciprocated the compliment by shifting her hip and posing. "Why thank you. Just a little something I threw together."

Edith's expression changed back again. She shot her hands at Lenore. Green beams flew at Lenore, but she tucked and rolled across the floor. A green blast obliterated the space she had left.

"Kill her!" Edith shouted.

Three salt people attacked Lenore with swords, but she was more skilled, and as her sword made contact, salt flew, and bodies crumbled.

Meanwhile, the birds interfered on Johnny's behalf. Johnny recovered and ran toward Edith, his sword raised. Demetrius ran to intercept him. Edith shot another beam, but it missed him again. However, it hit Mr. Buggins in midflight. He turned into salt and smashed into pieces against the wall. Lenore paused to watch the perishing bird. Chinwag and Nimoy attacked Edith to distraction. Demetrius met Johnny, and the two exchanged a series of violent blows. However, after several seconds, Demetrius was shattered into an expanding heap.

"Hurry, Johnny!" Lenore exclaimed. "I have the horses outside!" They ran out the doorway, smashing through resistance along the way. Nimoy and Chinwag flew outside after them. Edith shot at them from behind. Many of the salt people outside were confused by the noise and the sight of Johnny and Lenore fleeing out of the lodge. Johnny bumped into one of them and shoved him away.

"The horses are around the bend!" Lenore shouted.

Edith ran out and shot at them, emerald beams glowing in the darkness. Nimoy and Chinwag dove into her to distract her. Edith waved them off with frustration. "Don't just stand there, get them!" she yelled. "He must not escape. Get me a horse!" Some of the salt ran away from her around the other side of the lodge. The rest chased after Lenore and Johnny on foot. Moments later, a team of four horsemen brought a horse for her. She leaped onto it, and they galloped down the road.

It was dark, but Johnny and Lenore could make out the road beneath their feet. Johnny's sword also shone brightly. "The light," Lenore said when they reached the horses. "Sheath your sword!" He did so. Then they leaped onto their horses and galloped away before those chasing them on foot caught up to them.

At the speed they were going, the pathway was unclear in the darkness. Lenore rode in front. Their horses bobbed their heads, and their bodies stretched as their hooves pounded the road beneath them. Just as they turned another bend, a green flash flew past Johnny and hit a tree. The tree's trunk glazed into salt. Edith and her salt horsemen were behind them.

"Hurry, Johnny, the path out of here is just ahead! Oh!" Lenore veered quickly to avoid a small boulder sticking out along the edge of the path. It was too late for Winds. He leaped over it instead. Johnny wasn't prepared for the jump. When Winds landed, Johnny's body slammed into the saddle. He twisted to the side, grabbing the saddle horn, and pulling himself back up straight. As they rode under the sign with the ranch's name on it, another green flash flew past them. They galloped down the road into the night.

Edith and her horsemen pulled up short of the sign. However, one of the horsemen did not. As the horseman crossed, he cried out with terror, and he and the horse disintegrated into a ball of flame.

"Johnny!" Edith screamed. "Come back! It doesn't have to be this way! Johnny!"

Johnny and Lenore continued to ride, putting distance between them and the ranch. Edith's voice echoed her desperate rage into the night air. Finally, Lenore slowed her horse to a walk, patting its mane. Johnny did the same.

"That was a close call, Johnny. After you left the cabin, I felt in my spirit I needed to pack our things and prepare the horses to leave. I'm glad I did."

"Well, I suppose I should be grateful. But you did lead us there in the first place," Johnny replied, his sour tone hanging in the air. Lenore said nothing in response.

The two walked their horses for a time. Neither of them said anything, both merely desiring to put some distance between them and the ranch, knowing that Edith and her companions could not follow them. He drew his sword to provide some light. Johnny was tired, and he believed Lenore was as well. After a while, they found a patch of grass off to the side where they could hunker down to rest until morning. They unrolled their bags over the frosty dew and slept.

Chapter Six

THE EASIER PATH

Johnny slept hard. The morning sun had risen. His consciousness awakened before his eyes opened. His mind searched for the possibility that everything had been a dream, and he would wake up in the small apartment with Amanda nearby. But the warmth of his body inside the sleeping bag contrasted with the chill on his face from the frosty air. His thoughts recovered as he remembered the events of the previous night. He ventured to open his eyes against the morning sunlight. When he did, his eyes adjusted to the image of Lenore several feet away.

She was facing away from him, petting her horse's nose. Her tweed grey-and-powder-blue blazer matched the tweed Yorkshire driving cap and scarf. She wore light blue fitted jeans that painted the shape of her legs into brown leather boots. Her hair was laid back into a loose braid behind her. Johnny sat up in his sleeping bag and inhaled the brisk air.

Lenore turned and looked back at him. "You're up. Good morning. I was going to wake you earlier, but I didn't want to disturb your rest." She walked around the horse and continued to pet it. Are you hungry? I have a few treeperklyns left."

He nodded, although he still had rations. "But I need to relieve myself first," Johnny said.

She waved to an area where he would not be out in the open and politely turned around to give him some privacy. "We're not far from the base of the Great Valley, Johnny. The road forks ahead, and it's a half a day's ride down to the base of it."

"I'll be done soon!" Johnny shouted back not wanting to have the conversation while he was busy.

When Johnny was finished, he walked over to check on Winds, who was grazing nearby. He removed his canteen and took a drink. He then poured some water on his hands and wiped them on his pants. Lenore got a treeperklyn and handed it to him. "I'm sorry about Mr. Buggins. I feel bad about it. He was trying to protect me."

"Yes," Lenore replied, taking off her hat and holding it over her heart. "Mr. Buggins was a good bird who ate a lot of critters. May his transition to bird heaven be full of tasty creepy-crawlies and much bliss. May he rest in peace." Lenore put her hat back on, tossed her scarf over her shoulder, and walked back to her horse. "We can leave as soon as you're ready."

Johnny thought she would be more heartbroken about Mr. Buggins, but she was not. Noticing Lenore's new outfit yet again, Johnny waved his hand toward her. "Where could you have possibly gotten that outfit from? All of that couldn't come from your bag."

Lenore turned back to him. "I know, Johnny. I can't help it. It's an illness I have. I have a chronic fashion condition," she whispered as if embarrassed.

"My clothing hasn't changed much, but I have. I can handle the sword as good if not better than you now. And I'm becoming smarter about things."

"Smarter about what things, Johnny?"

"The mysterious man for starters."

Lenore put her head down and rubbed her thumbs together. "I'm sorry. I'm not allowed to say anything right now. But I do want to help you get home." She turned to the side. "I admit I've enjoyed having you around. It's been a great adventure so far, hasn't it?" she asked sheepishly.

"I think I've had enough of this adventure. I want it to end," Johnny replied. Nimoy perched next to him and clicked his head back and forth. "What about you, Nimoy? What do you have to say about all this?"

Nimoy merely flapped his wings and squawked.

"Since when are you at a loss for words?"

Nimoy repeated his squawking. Chinwag flew overhead doing the same. It came to mind that he had not heard any of them talk for some time. He turned back to Lenore with an inquisitive look. "Why aren't they talking?"

Lenore mounted her horse. "They only talked before because they were with me. However, they no longer follow me. They follow you now."

Johnny mounted his horse too. "They are? I don't understand. What does following someone have to do with anything?"

"They can talk, but they choose not to." She pulled the reins to lead her horse to the road, then gently pressed her heels into its sides. Johnny did the same and led Winds to continue their trek.

The two rode until they reached the fork in the road. From their view they could see the landscape of the distant valley and even farther out to the mountain, which was their destination. One path led down into the valley, and the other appeared to go around the mountain off to the right. Even from a distance, the valley appeared to be a desolate place. The other path appeared to have more shrubbery and growth from what the eye could see.

"There it is on the other side, Johnny. The mountain where the Great Door appears." She nodded down toward the valley. "The temperature down there is still cold, but it's very dry."

"What about this other path?" Johnny asked. "Does it connect around to the other side of the mountain?"

"Yes, but it's not your path."

"But if we can go around it. That would be better, right? It seems like it's a better route. We can have an easier time rather than going through that desolate place."

"But Johnny, we have to go through the valley," Lenore pleaded. "The easier way or the quickest route is not always the best."

"Is there danger on the higher path? Is there something you want to warn me about?"

"No, I don't know if there is or not."

"And the valley, what about the valley? Is there danger in the valley?"

"I hope not. It's a more difficult trek, but I don't think it's any more dangerous."

"I'm tired of making things more difficult. I should have taken up Daizel's offer to ride over on one of the bees. I'm sure we could have worked something out." He pointed to the upper road. "I'm going this way."

"But Johnny, it's not the right way."

"I have a right to choose, and I choose this way!"

"Trust me, Johnny. We need to go through the valley."

Johnny sat up tall in his saddle. "I'm going this way," he said, pointing. "I don't believe you anymore, and I don't trust you. I will lead the way. You can join me or not. I need to hurry and get over there to that mountain and go home!"

He turned Winds and started up the high road. The birds flew around after him. He looked back to see if Lenore was following. She was not. "You're not coming?" he asked.

"I cannot," Lenore said, shaking her head sadly.

"Maybe I'll see you over the mountain then. If not, thanks for your help."

"Johnny…" She reached out for a second but said no more, her eyes watering. Johnny looked back and saw her watching him ride around the bend. Then Lenore lowered her head and rode down the other path into the valley.

As Johnny rode, the surroundings were much the same as before. The sun had melted away the morning frost, but the chill remained. The air was fresh. Johnny and Wind's warm breath dissipated into small puffs of vapor. The light blue sky had barely a cloud above. The birds darted playfully back and forth. The trail ventured away from the valley closer to the forested hills on the other side of it. The only sounds were the occasional squawking of the two birds and the stomping of Winds' hooves.

Johnny had a different view of the awesomeness of the landscape than he had before. Home didn't compare to it. All of nature seemed to be catering to him. He didn't feel like a little boy; he felt strong and in control. He held his head high as Winds pranced under him. Riding Winds, with his mighty sword sheathed at his side, was the proudest he had ever felt. He was important in this place. Edith's question about why he wanted to return home rather than stay in Imagatorium rang in his mind.

Maybe Amanda doesn't care that I'm missing. Maybe they all would be better off without me. Maybe this isn't such a bad place after all.

He gave minor thought to Lenore choosing not to come with him. He had followed her way ever since he arrived. *She could have deferred to me this once, but she kept secrets, and I can't trust her.*

Chinwag and Nimoy flew ahead. Hours had passed, and it was now late morning. Trees lined the road on either side. Fading light shone through gaps in the towering trees, creating patches of shadow all around him. The trees stood still, but their branches swayed in the chilly breeze. He heard a rushing stream that had yet come into view. It was accompanied by the sound of many birds chirping and whistling.

His head snapped up at the sound of a boisterous squawk. He presumed it was Chinwag. However, his eyes met several crows gazing down at him with interest. Their feathers were glazed over like velvet. One of the crows squawked again, and other crows lifted their raspy voices in response. He became conscious of another murder of crows gathered in a nearby tree. They squawked and dithered around. Some differing species were intermingled with them, including magpies and ravens. As he looked around, he spotted Nimoy amongst them on one of the branches. Johnny saluted Nimoy and then continued down the road.

Minutes later, the stream came into view, swishing over rocks. He figured it was as good a place as any to take a break to fill his canteens.

He dismounted and then knelt beside the stream. The sound of water splashing and rolling over rocks filled his ears. He submerged the first canteen under the water and filled it up. He stopped to take a drink, then put the cap back on and began to fill the other. He noticed that the water was suddenly the only sound filling his ears. The squawking of the birds had ceased. Johnny put the cap on the second canteen and looked around him. Several birds were gathered. Despite the strangeness of them crowding him, Johnny felt comfortable. One walked up next to him as if curious to see what he was doing. It cocked his head and blinked.

"Look at you, Mr. Crow. You look like Chinwag. Are you two related?" The bird opened its beak and tilted its head. Johnny chuckled. He stood up and loaded the canteens back in his bag. When he mounted the horse, the birds made room for him to continue.

For several minutes other birds flocked around him. However, at a certain point, they ceased as if he had crossed some imaginary line that they could not follow.

He looked back. They filled the area behind him. Johnny shrugged and proceeded ahead.

As time passed, the road narrowed further. Up ahead he noticed something on the road. As he drew closer, he realized it was a child, a little girl maybe four or five years younger than him. She was African American, and her hair was braided in cornrows that dangled past her shoulders. She wore green leggings and a matching sweater with gold sequins embedded in it. Her tennis shoes were white and appropriate for a child of her age. She was sitting with her head down and her hands in her lap, her legs crossed in front of her. Her eyes were closed, and a staff was laid out beside her.

Winds slowed to a halt several feet in front of her even though Johnny had not pulled on the reins. He looked around, wondering if maybe an adult was nearby, but he didn't see anyone.

"You there, what are you doing on the road? Who's watching over you?"

The little girl slowly lifted her head and opened her eyes, staring up at him. "Maybe it's me who should ask you. What are you doing on this road, and who is watching over you?"

Johnny laughed at her sassiness. "I'm headed to the other side of the mountain." He looked around once more. "Is there a village nearby where you live?"

"No."

"Well, do you need any help then?"

"No, I do not," she replied. "But it looks like you do."

"Everything is fine with me," Johnny said. "Since everything is fine with you as well, may I ask you to move to the side of the road, so that I can pass?"

"No, you may not," the little girl replied. She yawned and stretched her arms, then grabbed her staff that had been lying on the ground beside her and stood up. She held the staff to the side and placed her other hand on her hip. "Turn around. Go back where you came from. This is not your path."

Johnny was taken aback by the girl's gall. "I'm trying to go back where I came from. I'm trying to go home."

"Not this way you're not," she replied.

"Are you trying to pick a fight or something? Do you own this path?" The little girl merely stared at him. Johnny rolled his eyes in exasperation. He nudged the sides of his horse to get him to move, but Winds refused. Finally, Johnny dismounted and pulled the reins, but Winds pulled his head back. "What's gotten into you,

Winds?" Johnny whispered. He decided to let the horse be for the moment and walked up to the little girl.

"Do you know who I am?" He patted the sword sheathed at his side. "Do you know what this sword has been through these past few days?"

The little girl chuckled. "Does the big man want to attack a little girl? It doesn't matter what you did in the past. It only matters what you are now and what you do in the future. I know who you are better than you do, it seems. And you're on the wrong path."

"Does this path lead to where the Great Door appears?"

"It does."

"That's where I'm headed."

"I know."

"Then why do you keep saying I'm on the wrong path?"

"Because you are."

"Well, I've had enough of this. I'm passing through."

"You cannot pass," the girl replied. She used her staff to draw a line in the dirt in front of her. She took a few deliberate steps backwards and then faced him again.

Johnny shook his head and laughed to himself. Then he walked back and mounted Winds again. He didn't want to hurt the girl, but he figured there was nothing she would be able to do to stop him on the horse. She would have to step aside. He kicked Winds' sides, and the horse reluctantly complied.

However, the second Winds stepped over the line, the girl reacted faster than Johnny was able to comprehend. She twirled several feet into the air and smacked Johnny in the side of his face with her staff. He flew out of the saddle. Just before he hit the ground, it opened to receive him and splashed as if he had plunged into water. The little girl landed on her feet, her body shifting with the waves until the ground settled. Winds recoiled back several feet away under her glare. She crouched down and assumed her previous seated position.

Although nothing visually around him suggested it, Johnny felt like he was suspended in a liquid gel. He could breathe normally, but he was floating in a murky nothingness. His hair swayed back and forth on top of his head. He moved his arms and felt resistance against his movements, his limbs moving slower than he liked. He instinctively looked up, as one would when attempting to swim to the surface while underwater, but he did not see a surface.

"Hello!" he cried. His voice was muffled as if underwater. "OK, you made your point. Can you get me out of here? Hello?"

There was no response. He had been floating there for several moments when he saw something tumbling toward him. It was a mirror. It grew larger and larger until he realized it was full length. As it slowed in front of him, he looked at his reflection and realized half of himself was missing, like the people he had met before.

"Nobody loves you at home," his reflection said. "You need to accept that and be content with it. You don't need anybody to care for you. You can make it all by yourself."

A loud voice competed in his mind with an answer. It was Lenore's voice. *"Everyone needs to love and to be loved, Johnny. I love you. Amanda loves you too. She needs you as much as you need her. Stay strong, Johnny. Understand the Book, and be careful of what people say, even yourself."*

The mirror continued past him and faded away. It was replaced with the floating image of Edith. Her alluring green eyes fixed on him. Her voice was soothing to his ear. "You can make it on your own. You can choose.

You can rule in Imagatorium. You will be worshiped here. Come back to me, Johnny. Release me from the boundaries of Zeboim. I will show you great mysteries and many comforts and pleasures."

"Don't listen to her," Lenore's voice interrupted. *"The allure of the salty woman of sin will slowly corrode your flesh and twist your vision. And without clear vision you will always return to the bondages of the past. Flee from the reach of her grip, and don't look back."*

The image of Edith faded.

A sweet floral array overtook his senses. He was enraptured by it. Flower petals drifted down. He saw Ratta Tootle and Gredo Graddle sitting quietly by a fire, enjoying each other's company. The petals rained heavily until the two of them disappeared.

Then he saw the stinger of a bee and the destructive venom of a beetle amongst the floral showers. He could taste the metallic scent of blood amongst the sweetness. He saw an image of Daizel's spirit raising a knife out of anger and coming down on Rosedar.

"Resentment *and hatred are just lower passions of the spirit of murder. They lead to destruction. Their consequences bring forth the greatest pain. When such blood is shed, its thirst won't be quenched. It brings no relief. Love and caring for one another is the greatest gift,"*

Lenore's voice said. *"It brings the greatest pleasure. It gives comfort during hard times."*

He suddenly saw Lenore through the eyes of an infant. She held him securely and pressed the nipple of a warm bottle to his lips. He readily suckled the milk from it. Lenore smiled and giggled with delight. She kissed his forehead and rocked him back and forth while he drank. His eyes became heavy, and he drifted off to sleep.

Then he was caught by another vision. He stood and watched Amanda beside the bed of her husband, who had just died. She wept and trembled, grabbing his shirt. She turned and looked past Johnny as if he was not in the room. In her eyes Johnny saw fear and despair.

Johnny felt a rush of air. It was followed by a stench. A deep, sinister laugh followed. Suddenly, he was face to face with the stronghold. Johnny turned away from the reptile's warm, rancid breath. The stronghold peered at Johnny with a look of lustful murder. "I'm back, Johnathan," the stronghold snarled. "You see, I agree with your flesh that you're an abandoned soul. You're nothing but a burden. You belong to me. You always have, and you always will. I own you." Imps appeared and darted around the stronghold. "You're who I say you are," the stronghold repeated through clenched teeth.

"Resist strongholds, Johnny. The battles you fight won't be against flesh and blood but the powers and principalities of the spirit."

The stronghold turned with a huff and flew away. However, the imps lingered.

Johnny saw an image of a young man facing away from him. The man was naked and holding his arms out to his sides, his palms toward the sky. The imps circled him. As Johnny looked closer, the imps turned into blackbirds, the majority being crows. The birds were unbridled and wild. The young man began to fade into a translucent state. In a confused whirlwind, the birds flapped around and clumped together where the body was disappearing. They formed into the shape of the vanishing young man, exactly as he had been standing. The atmosphere dimmed. A sheathed sword appeared at the young man's side. Still facing away from Johnny, he unsheathed the sword and appeared to look back over his shoulder.

Johnny felt a tinge of fear. Then his body was jerked upward, and he was compelled back to the surface.

Johnny shot out of the ground and several feet into the air, then crashed back down to the earth. He was soaking wet. He immediately felt the wind chill to his body. As he gathered his bearings, he wiped some of the dirt away that had caked on his face from the landing. He rubbed his chin and winced, reminded of the bruise on his cheek from the little girl's staff.

He looked around and saw her still sitting in the middle of the road. However, now they were at the fork in the road where he had parted with Lenore. Winds was happily eating a cluster of apples that were laid out before him on the grass. No birds were in sight. Johnny gathered himself and stood with a shiver.

The little girl pointed to the side of the road with her staff. "There's a towel and a change of clothes over there."

"Thank you," he said timidly. He walked over to a neatly folded towel and fresh clothing that included socks and shoes. Winds had apparently lost his fear of the little girl and paid Johnny no mind. Johnny changed his clothes, hesitating only for a moment out of modesty. When he was done, he put his wet clothes in a bag that was provided. Drying his hair with the towel, he walked over to Winds, who lifted his head to meet him. Johnny patted the bridge of his nose. Then he packed the wet clothes into a satchel and turned back to the little girl.

"How did we end up all the way back here?"

"Well, I rode Winds here," the little girl said. "We have an understanding now. As for you, you were meant to be here again."

"I see," Johnny responded. "But we were hours away. How long was I down there?"

"You have been away a full circle of the night and day, a little more than twenty-four hours, I suppose."

"Twenty-four hours?"

"A little more..."

"But why am I here, back at the fork in the road?"

The little girl stood and pointed her staff at him. "Must we go through this again?"

Johnny held the palm of his hands up. "No, no... That won't be necessary." He pointed to the path leading into the valley. "I'm going that way."

The little girl twirled her staff back to her side. "Smart boy. I knew you would get it eventually."

Winds had finished his small feast. Johnny approached him again. "Traitor," he whispered jokingly.

Winds shook his head in satisfaction. Johnny mounted him, then pulled the reins to move him back onto the road.

The little girl moved to the side, allowing them to pass.

He stopped beside her. "You're not going to say anything about what just happened to me? You aren't even going to give me an explanation?"

She shook her head slowly. "No."

"Well, is there anything else I should know?"

"Yes," she said, placing her hand on her hip. "Since you asked nicely, I'll tell you. You'll need the escort of an army to get through the valley."

"An army?"

"It's your path."

"And where am I supposed to get an army?"

"All that you need will be provided as long as you keep to the path provided for you." She shooed him with a flick of her wrist. "Move along now. Our time is over here."

Johnny smirked. "Who are you, exactly?"

"That's not important. Move along."

Johnny shook his head. Then he pressed his heels into Winds' sides to move him forward. After several paces down the road, he looked back at her. With her staff in hand, she turned and walked in the opposite direction, fading away into a dim light.

Johnny turned forward and proceeded down into the valley.

Chapter Seven

THE DRY VALLEY

ooking down from the plush mountain, a grim fog draped the valley's surface. Johnny descended toward the depths of the valley. The cool, stale air smacked in his mouth. He no longer could see the other side of the mountain, his visibility limited to about a hundred feet ahead. Vegetation became sparser. Winds continued ahead at a steady pace. Puffs of dust kicked from his horse's hooves.

Johnny had journeyed for more than an hour when he noticed something peculiar on the side of the road: a shield partially covered with dirt. A spear was nearby, sticking out at an angle from the ground. Close to it was a human skull. It lay detached from its ribcage and several other scattered bones. Amongst the bones was discarded weaponry, helmets, and military gear apparently from an army massacred and left to the elements long ago.

As Johnny rode, he continued to see similar debris. The valley was littered with greaves, coats of mail, swords, breastplates, and shields intermingled with parched and detached skeletal carcasses. The roadway became impeded, and he had to maneuver Winds through the dusty carnage.

Johnny noticed a figure curled up on the ground. It was different from the dryness of stale death around him. It was not of dry bones but flesh, the discarded body of a woman. He panicked at first, thinking it was Lenore, but the woman had a different build. She was wearing a white dress. Johnny considered that maybe the woman could be alive, so he called out to her, but there was no response. He dismounted and approached her. But when he saw who it was, he jumped back, shrieking in horror. Staring back at him with a blank expression was his adopted mother, Amanda.

"Mom!"

A whirlwind overtook him and pushed him back. He covered his face. The rising sand engulfed Amanda's body. Her flesh faded to bones and then melded into the twirling dust. The whirlwind became stronger, lifting the empty dress within its vortex and carrying it away.

Johnny extended his arm and shouted his mother's name. Then he fell to his knees and wept.

He stayed there for several minutes. He then mounted his horse and continued; his head hung low. Johnny knew it was only a vision. Amanda hadn't really just turned to dust and floated away in the parched whirlwind. However, it still shook him.

His time in Imagatorium had made him think he could stand up and do things himself and maybe make a difference in life. He could lead and not be a follower. But in doing so, he also was learning that he needed to be humble, or he would be humbled.

As these thoughts faded from his mind, he heard a woman humming and singing in the fog. As he drew closer to it, he realized it was Lenore.

She came into view. She was sitting on the ground clanking the top of a helmet with two bones. Inside the helmet was a human skull. Her horse was standing several feet away. Chinwag stood next to her, panting, his beak open to the rhythmic sounds.

"The ankle bone connected to the leg bone. The leg bone connected to the hip bone. The hip bone connected to the, uh... middle bones..."

Despite the somber environment, Johnny couldn't help but smile at her.

Upon seeing him, Lenore held the back of her hand to her forehead and wailed in an exaggerated fashion. "Weeping and lamentations!" she cried. "Woe is me! Johnny left me in the valley all by myself with this cranky bird that refuses to talk to me anymore." Chinwag squawked in protest. With the parched bones in her hands, she continued with a drum roll. "And thus, comes a second woe." She paused and hunched over. "Woe is me."

Johnny stopped his horse next to her. Lenore looked up at him coyly. "Oh, it's you." She smirked. "You're not still mad at me, are you, Johnny?"

He chuckled and dismounted. "What happened here? What is this place?"

"It's the Valley of Defeat and Despair. It's said that a great army was defeated here. The victors slaughtered them, not leaving one alive. They took care of their own but left the defeated corpses to rot in the valley."

Lenore stood up. As she did, the skull rolled out from under the helmet. She looked down at it. "Wild animals of the earth, the fowl of the air, bugs, and larvae fed on their bodies. All that's left are dried and scattered bones... Here lies hopelessness. Here lies the broken dreams of many."

Lenore picked up the skull and gazed into its eye sockets. "I wonder what color his eyes were. This one once had a tongue that could speak and maybe even sing. This was somebody's son. This was someone's memory long gone." She took a closer look at the skull and then struck a pose like an actor on stage. "Let me see. Alas, poor Yorick. I knew him, Horatio, a fellow of infinite jest, of most excellent fancy. And now how abhorred in my imagination it is. My gorge rises at it."

Johnny peered at Lenore, begging a question with his eyes. "Did you ever plan on telling me?" Johnny asked.

Lenore ceased her recitation of Shakespeare to look at him.

"Why didn't you tell me who you were in the beginning? Why didn't you tell me you were my mother?"

Lenore returned his stare with warmth and fear. "I really wanted to, but if I told you then you would have never accomplished what you were meant to." Her eyes filled with tears. "I longed to embrace you and call you, my son."

Johnny came over and hugged her. Tears rolled down her cheeks as she returned his embrace.

"Why did you leave me?"

"Oh, dear Johnny, I never left you. In your world my life ended. I'm only here in Imagatorium to help you fulfill your purpose."

"You can't go back with me?"

Lenore shook her head. "You don't understand. I'm always with you." She pointed to his chest. "Imagatorium is a place that is inside of you. You were a boy, and you will grow up to be a good man. You have traits in you that people will need. You may not understand it now, but Amanda needs you too. You're a leader. It's already inside of you. You must overcome the obstacles that will come against you, as you have done here."

Johnny didn't care to untangle all that Lenore had just said. It was enough to welcome the long overdue hug from his mom.

While they were hugging each other, they heard the faint and steady clanging of a bell. It was coming out of the fog from the road ahead of them. They both stood back. The sound increased in volume. Johnny looked at Lenore, curious about what was coming their way. Then a man appeared through the fog. Johnny placed his hand on the hilt of his sword.

"I don't think you'll need your sword, Johnny."

It was an old man with a long staff. His tunic was loose fitting, and the top of his head was bald. His remaining gray hair was wild and disheveled. His face was serious, and his beard was short and scraggly. The clanging came from a cowbell attached to his backpack. To Johnny, he looked like a crazy homeless man.

"It's old man Zeke," Lenore whispered. "At least he's walking around with his clothes on this time." She circled her finger by her temple to indicate he was a little strange.

Zeke stopped in front of them. However, his eyes looked past them as if he was connected to something else.

"Zeke, it's nice to see you," Lenore said. "It's so nice that your hair and beard have grown back from the last time I saw you."

He retrieved several strands of hair that were tied together from inside his tunic and handed them to Johnny without looking at him directly. "This is for you."

Johnny recoiled from the man.

"Just take it," Lenore whispered.

He did so.

Finally, the old man focused his eyes on Johnny. "Son of man, what is it that you see here in this valley?"

Johnny contemplated the man's question, looking around briefly before he responded. "I see a fog that impairs our vision. I see death from a defeated army from times past. I see what's left, dry, scattered bones."

"Son of man, can these bones live?"

What kind of question is that? Johnny wondered.

"I don't know, sir, but I sense that you do."

"Son of man, speak to these bones. Say to them, 'O dry bones, hear the Word of the Lord. The Lord will cause breath to enter you. The Lord will put ligaments, muscle, and flesh on you and cover you with skin; and you shall live.'"

Johnny looked at Lenore, who shrugged. He felt silly talking to scattered bones, but decided to go along with it, repeating the old man's words.

As he finished speaking, he heard a rumbling sound. Bones rattled and rose from the earth. Then they began to attach themselves to each other.

Lenore ducked as a femur flew over her head.

Skeletal forms began to merge around them. Johnny watched closely as ligaments and muscles covered the skeletal forms. When the flesh was complete, the bodies were suspended upright.

Military clothing and weaponry began to cover them. When the process was complete, their bodies descended to the ground. Johnny noted that their eyes were closed, and they did not appear to be breathing or alive. He turned back to the old man as if expecting more.

"Son of man, speak to the four winds, and tell them to breathe on these, who have been slain, that they may live."

Johnny did so.

It started as a breeze, but then it felt like the wind kicked up from different directions, blowing at them from all sides. One by one the bodies took a deep breath and opened their eyes. Finally, they stood upright, a great army.

The old man turned to Johnny again. "You can bring life to that which is dry, dead, and hopeless. Live your life accordingly." He turned and continued up the road.

The army formed into brigades and stood at attention. The soldiers were silent, but for the barking of orders of their commanders. They formed lines in front and behind them and readied themselves to march.

"The little girl said I would need the escort of an army to get through the valley. I guess this is it."

"Little girl?" Lenore asked.

"The little girl who told me I was on the wrong path."

"Oh?"

"Don't tell me you don't know about her."

She waved her hand. "OK, I won't tell you that, but I don't know what you're talking about. It doesn't matter anyway. We're on the right path now." She winked. "Shall we proceed, Johnny?"

"Yes, Mother, let's proceed." He mounted his horse.

Lenore smiled and went to mount her horse as well. On the way, she stopped to look at one of the soldiers. "Brown, Johnny. Yorick's eyes are brown." She left the soldier to mount her horse.

The army marched ahead of them for the rest of the day until darkness began to fall. They finally set up camp, knowing that in the morning they would reach the other side and start their assent out of the valley. Johnny knew that would mean they would soon part for good. He felt uneasy, knowing it would not be as simple as marching up to the Great Door and saying their goodbyes. *After all, why would we need to have an army escort just to do that?*

The early morning sun reflected an array of orange through a draping haze. The campfire from the night before had dwindled to embers. Guards were awake and standing at attention. However, Johnny and Lenore were still asleep.

Johnny's nose twitched as a whiff of foul air touched his senses. It was a familiar smell. He opened his eyes and saw Chinwag and Nimoy looking at him. As he stared into their eyes, he could feel the seriousness they projected. It was not a product of fear but of something else. He sensed the birds were about to leave for good. After a few moments, the two birds unceremoniously flew away into the morning fog. Meanwhile, soldiers began to bustle around.

Lenore woke up and scrunched her face. Closing her eyes again, she let out a deep sigh.

"It's back," Johnny grumbled. He rose and flicked his wrist, then retrieved his sword. "I'm better prepared to face him now, and we have a sizable army with us this time."

"I'm glad you've developed optimism, Johnny." She also reached for her sword. "We're going to need it. It smells like that funky lizard has brought along a couple of his friends this time."

They both fell silent and listened. Through the foggy mist came the beasts' taunting roars. Johnny breathed in the sulfuric funk of their decadence and winced. An army commander came to him with his sword drawn.

Others were behind him. The commander held his sword toward Johnny's. Johnny tapped his sword to his. A spark ignited around the swords' edges. The commander turned to the others and tapped his sword to theirs, who passed it down the line. Lenore tapped her sword against Johnny's as well. They all raised their glowing swords and waited.

The same grey beast as before appeared out of the haze. It flew past them, bellowing. The downdraft from its wings was repressive, causing some of those below to lose their balance. The grey beast was followed by a black beast, which was about the same size, and then a smaller brown beast. Filth and rancidness trailed behind them.

The fluttering sound of shadow imps followed the beasts. Johnny raised his sword against the onslaught. However, what came amongst them was more disturbing. Black-armored half souls wielding their swords. Like before, their movements were like that of a whole person, but they were not. They were half people, some visible on the left side and some on the right. However, they weren't apathetic and disinterested as before. They moved as one with anger and hatred.

The soldiers engaged. Most wielded their swords with confidence, striking down imps and half people alike.

However, Johnny took special note of one of the resurrected soldiers going off the path to meet the enemy. Doubt and fear were etched onto the soldier's face. A few moments later, the soldier was killed. He cried out and then disintegrated into nothingness. As Johnny looked around, he saw others fall to the attackers. *How can those who were just resurrected back to life die so soon?* he wondered.

Gathering his courage, he went out to engage the enemy forces. One of the soldiers stopped him and pointed to Lenore, who was on the pathway. She yelled back to him while mounting her horse. "Let's go, Johnny! Stay on the path. Come on!" She waved for him to follow her on the pathway.

Johnny's natural inclination was to ignore Lenore's voice and help fighting soldiers. *They're perishing because of me. They're laying down their lives to get me where I need to go even though they only just received their lives back yesterday. Why?*

Time froze. He turned and saw another one of his protectors perish at the hand of a half man. Inside him, wrath battled with fear. Amidst the turmoil of emotion,

Johnny realized that the imps were creating interference for the half soldiers, who struck from behind them.

Meanwhile, the deep rumble of hostility from the three beasts continued to cause distraction and echo terror throughout the valley. Their foul stench was unbearable. The beasts flew in low, bellowing at the half soldiers and the imps.

"Johnny!" Lenore exclaimed. "You must lead us forward!"

Winds galloped toward him, ready to be mounted. Johnny regathered himself and hopped on Winds, then rode down the path toward Lenore.

He led them at a slow trot because imps flooded the pathway. Half soldiers kept coming. They breached the ranks within the steady confusion of the imps.

"Focus beyond the imps!" Johnny shouted. "Don't go after the imps. Fight them off so you can see the halfers!"

With a wave of his sword, Johnny rushed Winds through a cluster of imps on the road. They parted, exposing a half soldier hidden behind them. Johnny swung his sword at the half soldier, causing him to disintegrate. He dispatched another in a similar manner. Soldiers began to crash into the imps' ranks, striking down the half soldiers concealed by them. Johnny returned to the path, continuing to fight his way forward.

After a time, the path started to ascend the mountain. As if reaching a hidden marker, trees and brush appeared on either side of the path. The top of the mountain became clearer, and the fog lessened.

The aggressiveness of the half men diminished until they were no longer engaging the soldiers. The imps fluttered away, many flying ahead of Johnny and Lenore. The three beasts flew past and thumped down on the path in front of them.

Johnny pulled Winds to a halt. Lenore and the army stopped as well. Cries of defiant fury thundered from the beasts' throats. Imps fluttered behind the beasts like bats. However, the boasts coming from the beasts became less and less intimidating to Johnny as he became focused on the strange reaction of the imps.

Then Johnny noticed a young man standing with his back to them on the pathway, facing the three beasts. He had a sword in his hand, and he was naked.

The young man held up his sword to the beasts, and at his command, they subdued their fury. Each bowed before the young man before fading away into nothingness. Then the young man, with his sword still raised, faded away like the beasts.

The imps began to change form and squawk. One by one they were transformed into black birds, the predominant one being a large crow. The birds descended toward the fading young man and attached themselves to where his body had disappeared. One by one they connected to him around his torso, limbs, and head. The squawking ceased as they attached.

When they finished, a dark, living silhouette put down his sword, and silence descended. He turned his head toward Johnny. He had no facial features, no eyes, and no mouth. The man walked toward the forested area just off the path, which was covered by a patch of dense fog.

Johnny knew he was supposed to follow. This was the figure that had trailed them from the beginning. He was part of Johnny's vision. It was the man of blackbirds and crows. He turned to Lenore with questions in his eyes.

Lenore sighed in response. "This is a confrontation I can't help you with, Johnny. There are some things that you must face all by yourself. I cannot go with you."

Johnny reasoned the challenge had to be that way. *So, this is my path.*

"But who is he?" Johnny asked. Lenore remained silent, merely nodding knowingly. Johnny held her stare for a few moments. "Then it will be what it will be." He dismounted. "I'll see what this crow man wants."

He looked back at Lenore and the army. Then he turned toward the conspicuous fog. Johnny gripped his sword and followed the Crowman inside.

Chapter Eight

THE CROWMAN

The Crowman disappeared into the dense fog amidst several trees. The fog looked denser than the fog on the path, as if it were an unnatural phenomenon. Once he got to the edge, Johnny paused to look around and listen. Then he proceeded with caution.

As he stepped in, he felt the heaviness of his surroundings pressing against his flesh. His eyes teared up. The wind sounded muffled in his ears. He braced himself against a tree. The branches and leaves wavered, and birds squawked in the distance. He struggled to fight off a spell of dizziness.

However, after a time, he began to adjust. Johnny squinted his eyes closed and then opened them again, only to see a large crow glaring at him like an intruder.

Immediately, he perceived the bird to be Chinwag. Chinwag sized Johnny up, then flew over to a nearby decaying tree that had fallen onto its side. Chinwag began to peck the bark, the sound echoing in Johnny's ears and increasing in volume.

Feeling suspicious, Johnny gripped his sword, but there was nothing but the wind and the tapping of the bird's beak against the bark. A beetle scampered across the trunk. Chinwag clamped down on the bug with his talons and snapped it. He chomped his beak until it was consumed. As Johnny stepped toward him, Chinwag looked up and shuffled his feet.

"So, Chinwag, have you left us to join the enemy? Are you now with this man full of birds?"

Chinwag merely turned his head to the side and returned to pecking at the bark. *Peck, peck, peck...*

"Where is he?"

Peck, peck, peck...

"What does he want?"

Peck, peck, peck...

The sound reverberated louder and louder.

Peck, peck, peck...

Johnny winced.

Peck, peck, peck...

Johnny slammed his sword onto the log. "Stop it, Chinwag. Stop it!"

Chinwag jumped up, his wings flapping, and flew away, squawking. The bird's voice soon blended with the other squawks coming from beyond. Johnny's eyes followed him in the fog until he disappeared. With his sword down to his side, he followed.

Suddenly, everything was silent. As Johnny rounded a tree, he kicked up discarded leaves with his feet. Some shuffled around him in the wind, which whispered his name. "Joooohnnnnyyyy..." The voice was deep, and it sent a chill throughout his body. However, Johnny wasn't going to be caught off guard by an ambush from the Crowman. He raised his sword as he continued to creep forward.

"Joooohnnnnyyyy..." this wind whispered again. This time it sounded more like a question.

Johnny felt another gust. Several more leaves swirled around him, joining together as a cluster.

The wind laughed, no longer a whisper. "Joooohnnnnyyyy..." it said, this time more confidently.

As he stepped closer to the cluster of leaves, he noticed it was not one cluster but several. He recoiled at the silhouettes of human figures within them.

The first shadow was that of a half soldier with a sword unsheathed at his side. A little farther away stood another. They were perfectly still. Johnny inched forward, preparing to do battle, but neither one responded. As he closed in further, he noticed that the figures were made entirely of leaves. The detail was such that Johnny could easily discern what the images were.

The first half soldier resembled the overseer. The second looked like Kenaniah. On the ground next to them, what Johnny initially thought was just a pile of leaves was actually a severed dragon claw. It was the same size as that of the stronghold.

He turned further to see the pristine but enraged image of Daizel. Several feet apart from her stood Queen Rosedar, who looked livid as she faced her. Behind them were images of some of their floral soldiers, Asteralians and roses alike. He saw a large bee and a beetle with them. It was impressed upon him that the rude banter and bickering in his world between Ms. Daisy and Ms. Rose were manifested in Imagatorium for what it really was, the spirit of hatred, envy, and murder. In Imagatorium their petty quarreling became plots of destruction and violent warfare.

Johnny continued to walk between them. Images of Gredo Graddle and Ratta Tootle stood holding hands.

He considered the love between them and the despair that Gredo Graddle felt when he thought he might have lost his soulmate.

Johnny came to the image of Edith. She stood seductively with her hand on her hip. Several others knelt before her. Some were prostrate on the ground in apparent worship. She represented the seduction of the world with all its passions. Its goal was power and control over its subjects. In the end, many willingly accepted her consequences. They also accepted the boundaries that they themselves had set in motion. In Johnny's world those things were subtle and difficult to detect. In Imagatorium the degenerative saltiness of their flesh was more defined.

Johnny looked beyond and found the image of the little girl with the staff. Her head was turned to the image of the old man, Zeke. They represented the hope of the future. It was to stay on the right path. It was the resurrection of the dead things in life.

Then there was the image of Lenore. Three leafy birds were perched on a tree branch above her head: Chinwag, Mr. Buggins, and Nimoy, who was made of orange leaves. The image of Lenore showed coyness and class, mystery, and intrigue. She was beautiful, witty, protective, and, at times, supernatural. Despite her nonsensical moments, he would have the image of his mother be no other way. When he looked at her with all her imperfections, his love for her never waned. He knew she only did what she believed was best for him. He had to get through his own doubts and fight off thoughts of rejection, abandonment, and distrust.

Then he saw a shadow seated against a tree. Unlike the other figures, this one moved. It appeared to be writing in a sketchbook. Taking a few steps closer, Johnny realized it was the Crowman. His initial thought was to brace for defense, but the Crowman made no movement toward him, though it was apparent that he knew Johnny was there. However, he still paid Johnny no mind. He just continued to scribble in the sketchbook.

Johnny circled widely around him. As he did, he noticed that several other sketchbooks spread out on the ground next to the Crowman. They were like the ones that Johnny used to sketch and doodle, the same brand that Amanda bought for him. Some were black, and some were green.

For someone who had lured him into a confrontation, the Crowman didn't appear to be taking this confrontation seriously. *Maybe he's just toying with my emotions and is overly confident. Maybe it's me that's supposed to initiate the confrontation.*

The Crowman closed the sketchbook and set it and the pencil down. Then he picked up his sword, stood up, and walked back toward the leaf statues. The Crowman turned his head toward Johnny as he passed, giving Johnny a closer view of the Crowman's face—or at least his head because he didn't really have a face.

Johnny started to follow, but he was curious about the sketchbooks. Something drew him to them, something familiar yet puzzling. *Does the Crowman want me to look at the sketchbooks? Is this part of my destiny? Part of my path? Or is this some sort of trap?* Johnny did not know for sure, but the mystery of the sketchbooks became increasingly overpowering. He had to see.

With one eye on the Crowman as he disappeared into the fog, he crept toward the sketchbooks and reached for one of them. He thumbed through the first few pages. The drawings inside were almost lifelike. They appeared to be a play-by-play of his time in Imagatorium. *The Crowman must have been following me the whole time and drawing my adventures in the sketchbooks, but why? What interest does he have in me?* He figured the other sketchbooks would be the same. He was curious to continue looking, but he became concerned about the Crowman's whereabouts, especially considering he was still unsure about his intentions.

He glanced around him to make sure he was not being approached. He knew he was taking a chance, but his thoughts returned to the sketchbook. *If this is his chronicle in Imagatorium, what's the Crowman's last entry?* He picked up the last book that the Crowman had put down and thumbed to the last drawing. He was mesmerized by it, but he also was confused. On one side of the page were images of the Crowman and Johnny amongst burning heaps, engaged in a fight with clashing swords. The last picture was of Johnny dressed like one of the half soldiers. However, he was two different halves. One half was Johnny, and the other half was the Crowman. The two images were merged.

Johnny's mind wandered. *Is this Crowman related to me? Lenore is my mother. Could this possibly be my father? Is this the secret that Lenore could not tell me?*

The voice in the wind interrupted his thoughts with a chuckle. *Listen to your heart, Johnny. You know I'm not your father. Now, enough of this; your time has come. You must face me.*

"Why?" Johnny yelled. "Why do I have to face you? I didn't ask for this!"

There was no response. Johnny was more confident than he had ever been in his life. However, the heaviness of fear hung in the air stronger than any foe in Imagatorium, including the stronghold. He knew the Crowman was someone he did not want to face.

He considered making a run for it up the mountain to the Great Door, but he surmised the Crowman would not let that happen. Everything had led up to this moment, and he did not know why. *Why go through all of this just to die at the hands of this freak of nature?*

"I have no quarrel with you!" he shouted.

Again, no response.

Just then the smell of smoke wafted through the air. Beyond the trees where the Crowman had disappeared, blurry flames flickered through the fog. Johnny readied his sword, which lit up and vibrated in anticipation of contact. He approached with caution.

The leaf figures were fully engulfed with flames. They burned with intense heat but did not appear to be consumed. The nearby trees were also unaffected. The fires were contained as if they were merely torches.

Amidst the swirling flames stood the Crowman. The brightness of his sword gleamed against the backdrop of misty orange. His head turned to follow Johnny's movements.

Johnny snapped his wrists and readied his sword for an attack. The Crowman did the same, mimicking Johnny's movements.

"What do you want from me?" Johnny asked. "I have no quarrel with you!"

The Crowman titled his head to the side and back again. Then he lifted his sword and charged. Defying gravity, he flew at Johnny, swinging his sword downward.

Johnny stepped sideways and met the Crowman's sword with an upward backhanded swing. A few birds attached to the Crowman's body separated and then quickly flew back into place.

Johnny rolled to his feet as the Crowman slid past and then turned to face him.

The Crowman did not attack right away; he merely paced back and forth as if measuring Johnny's resolve.

Johnny bore in and swung at him. The Crowman bent unnaturally backward, and Johnny's sword missed his chest by inches.

Johnny's next swing was met by the Crowman's sword, as was the next. Johnny lunged forward, and the Crowman again defied gravity by leaping upward and doing a backflip, landing with his feet on a tree trunk. The Crowman stood perpendicular to the ground above Johnny. Johnny swung upward, their swords clanging together.

The Crowman dodged one of Johnny swings by bending his knees and falling back against the tree.

He rolled around the tree to the other side as Johnny's sword chipped off pieces of bark where the Crowman vacated.

As Johnny stepped around the tree, the Crowman jumped to the ground behind the flaming pillar of the mammoth bee. Then he sprang out and charged Johnny again, their swords locking together.

The Crowman swung around and kicked Johnny in the chest. Upon contact, several birds exploded from the Crowman's leg. He held his leg up for a few moments until the birds returned to where they had separated.

Johnny crashed to the ground; the wind knocked out of him. Gasping for air, he writhed on his back and tried to get up. Any cockiness that Johnny might have felt before had vanished. He was hurt, but he knew if he did not get up soon, it would be the end of him. He lurched to his feet, taking short breaths.

The Crowman charged once again, forcing Johnny to fend off another flurry of blows. He yelled at the Crowman with each swing. Johnny did not know how he survived the next few moments, but somehow, he did.

Seeing that Johnny had recovered, the Crowman backed off. Johnny appreciated the momentary reprieve. He smirked at the Crowman with renewed confidence.

Then he narrowed his gaze, snapped his wrists, and stretched his neck to the side.

The Crowman mimicked Johnny by snapping his own wrists and stretching his neck to the side as well.

Eyeing the Crowman, Johnny held out his hand and shook the sword loosely to his side. The Crowman hunched down and again mimicked Johnny's movement.

Seeing the sword shake in the Crowman's grip, he noticed something that he had not noticed before. *The sword, it's the same. It's the same sword.*

Johnny's mind raced, jumping to the Crowman's mannerisms and the sketchbooks. He paused and stood upright, then dropped his sword to the side.

The Crowman stood upright as well.

"How can this be?" Johnny asked. "You're me, aren't you? I'm fighting against myself."

The Crowman held his sword to his chest and bowed in acknowledgement. Then he assumed a combative stance and, with his free hand, beckoned Johnny to continue.

"No, I won't. I will not fight against myself." Johnny took a few steps toward the Crowman and slammed his sword into the ground. "I release you. You're free."

The Crowman did not move for a moment. Then he pointed his sword at Johnny. Johnny closed his eyes. A few more moments passed. The Crowman slammed his sword into the ground a few feet from Johnny's.

The leaves ceased burning, and the leaf figures collapsed. The Crowman and Johnny looked back as a stream of light broke through the fog and beamed down on them. The Crowman turned back to face Johnny, held his fist to his chest, and bowed. Johnny watched as birds peeled off the Crowman and flew up into the sunlight. Johnny smirked as one of the birds, an orange one, flew around him and squawked before following the others into the sky.

"Goodbye Nimoy," he said warmly. The fog peeled back into the breaking sunlight. As the last of the birds flew away, the Crowman was no more.

Johnny looked at the two swords embedded in the ground facing each other. He would no longer need his sword in Imagatorium. Now he carried the sword of truth in his heart. It seemed fitting to let the swords stay where they were.

Just then, Lenore approached. "Johnny, I knew you could do it."

Johnny smiled. The fog lifted, revealing a path leading up the mountain. Through the dissipating fog, the Great Door came into view. They stood for a time holding hands and watching the fog disappear. Johnny felt the mother's love that he had never known before. He also felt a pang of sadness. He had reached his destination and would never see her again. It was time to go up the path and return to his own world.

Lenore squeezed his hand and her eyes watered. He could feel her hesitation. She took his arm in hers and kissed him on the cheek. Then they walked up the path, arm in arm.

"It's OK, Johnny. You fulfilled your destiny here. But your future is in your world."

A tear rolled down his cheek. "Will I ever see you again?"

She squeezed his arm. "Not this way, Johnny. Not until many years from now in the afterlife. When you go back, all this will seem like a dream, a very real dream. However, it is as real as the world to which you shall return. Imagatorium will be seared into your consciousness. You will overcome there because you will remember that you overcame here." She smiled. "Of course, you know that now."

The two continued to walk up the path. The door radiated brightness. As before, it stood all by itself, not attached to anything, a beautiful black door with gold trim and a golden handle.

When they were still several feet away, the door opened for them, revealing a bright light. A vision of Amanda appeared. She turned toward them and smiled warmly. Her face was full of peace and love. She went through the door and disappeared into the brightness.

"I've never seen her like that," Johnny said.

"Your presence will influence her to be the woman that you saw. Stay on the path, Johnny. Amanda needs you as much as you need her." She hugged Johnny and held him tight. "I'm proud of you, and I love you." She let him go and then nodded toward the door.

Johnny's eyes teared up.

"Go ahead, Johnny. I will always be with you."

Johnny took one last look at her and then approached the door. The light engulfed him, and Johnny departed Imagatorium.

CHAPTER NINE

NEW AWAKENING

Johnny felt a surge of warmth and comfort. It was as if God Himself had embraced him. He did not want to leave that moment, but he felt the sensation of a gentle breeze against his face and the rigidness of the tree against his back.

"Johnny!" Amanda called. He gradually opened his eyes, then sat up and wiped the tears from his cheeks. She knelt beside him and checked to see if he was injured. Then she brushed his hair back with her hand. "Are you OK? Did something happen?"

Johnny looked around. His sketchbook and pencil were beside him. "I must have fallen asleep." *But everything seemed so real. I couldn't have fallen asleep.*

"You scared me seeing you lying down like that." She used the back of her finger to wipe a tear from his eye. "Did you have a bad dream?"

"No." Johnny smiled. "It was a very good dream. Challenging but still very good."

"Well, you couldn't have been asleep for more than ten minutes or so."

"Only ten minutes?"

Amanda smiled and nodded. Johnny reached up and hugged her.

"Are you sure everything is alright, Johnny?"

He laughed. "Yes, Mom, everything is fine."

Amanda pulled back to look at him again. "Well, OK, we can pack some plates and go home if you want to. I'm sorry I didn't realize you were that tired before."

"No, Mom, we shouldn't go. We might be a blessing to someone if we stay."

Amanda stared at him for a few moments. "I guess I never thought of it that way, although I'm not sure how we can be a blessing to this group."

She helped Johnny to his feet. Johnny picked up his sketchbook and pencil. With her arm around him, they walked back to the others, who were waiting for them around the table.

"Is he alright, Amanda?" Pastor Jason called out.

"Yes, he's fine. He just fell asleep."

"Yes, something about that tree that lends itself to napping," Pastor Jason replied. "I've taken a few naps there myself." He winked at Johnny.

Zeke was at the table eating a slice of pie. "Want to try some of this apple pie? It's really good."

Johnny nodded eagerly.

"I'll get you a piece," Amanda sat.

Johnny sat at the table. The others gathered as Amanda set a slice of pie in front of him and then sat down.

"Thanks, Mom," Johnny said.

She smiled and nodded.

Johnny ate a piece and then nodded in approval. "It's to die for." He chuckled under his breath.

"It's store bought, but it still has a good taste to it," Zeke said from across the table. He chewed another piece. "Did you draw anything else in your book while you were over there?"

"Not really," Johnny said, smiling. "I didn't draw anything new, but I did think a lot about my drawings."

"Oh?" Amanda replied.

"Did you decide to draw some roses?" Rose asked.

Daisy rolled her eyes.

"No," Johnny replied. "It occurred to me that drawing flowers is the grimmest of all."

"How so?" Pastor Jason asked.

"Well, a whole lot of flowers are given when somebody dies. Like at my father's funeral. There were flowers everywhere. But no matter the beauty and the scents coming from them, it could not cover the fact that he was dead, and my mother and I were hurting." He reached out and squeezed Amanda's hand. "It's like a mask. Sweet words are spoken, but the flower covers up what's really in our hearts."

He glanced at Rose and then at Daisy, who was standing next to Pastor Jason. "In the same way, we can hide what's really in our hearts by the sweet fragrances of what we say and do. People can show love but not mean it, so I figure that makes it the grimmest of all."

Amanda smiled warmly at him. "I didn't know you felt that way."

Everyone was silent for several awkward moments until Zeke rescued them. "What about the drawings you showed us earlier? How about the dragon? Tell me about the dragon."

Johnny laughed at Zeke's enthusiasm, as did the others. Johnny opened his sketchbook and turned to the page with the drawing of the dragon. "It represents a stronghold that stands in our way. It's a foul power. I guess we all have to face one at one time or another." He caught Edith's eye. She was listening intently to what he was saying. He turned back to Ken. "It's that thing you know shouldn't be in your life, but it claims it owns you. It's too big and scary to fight and maybe even comfortable to us, but we must resist it, and it has to flee." He turned to Pastor Jason. "You said that didn't you, Pastor?"

"Well, yes, Johnny, I guess I did."

Zeke laughed. "Pastor, you preached that sermon over a year ago!"

"Yeah, well at least somebody was listening," Pastor Jason joked.

"I remembered it too, you know," Zeke replied.

"I suppose you did," Pastor Jason said.

"Wow, a lot has come out of that mind of yours after that little nap you took," Edith said.

"I guess my nap cleared my head, so I could focus on what's important in life."

Edith snickered uncomfortably.

Pastor Jason looked over at the basketball lying on the grass. "Hey Johnny, are you up for a game of Horse?"

"I'm in!" Ken said.

"I've seen you shoot. I don't even think prayer will help you," Pastor Jason replied.

Ken grinned. "I've been working on some trick shots."

Pastor Jason turned back to Johnny, who looked at Amanda for permission. She squeezed his hand and patted him on the back. Johnny got up from the table, his sketchbook in hand, and trotted over to pick up the ball.

"I'll join you," Zeke said.

Johnny stopped for a moment and returned to Amanda, handing her the sketchbook. "Can you hold onto this for me?"

She smiled warmly. "Yes, I'll keep it right here in my purse."

As the guys left to play Horse, Johnny looked around at the beautiful trees. Then he slowed down to glance at the fountain. The hedge that encircled it was neatly cut, and the leaves were bursting with the green vigor of life. The water spouted fresh and clear. A variety of birds gleefully splashed and enjoyed each other's company. Johnny chuckled to himself with the thought that the cement baby cherub might lift his head and wink at him.

The four of them gathered together in fellowship, Johnny enjoying the friendly banter with other men. They did not treat him like, nor did he feel like, a child anymore. For the first time in his life, he felt like one of the guys, a man amongst men.

CLOSING

A crow circled above four happy figures shooting baskets below. The crow squawked repeatedly and flapped its wings. It then soared over the church grounds and turned to fly north. After several moments, the crow spotted what it was looking for, and it began its descent. Other blackbirds joined it, gliding down together.

A dark figure waited for them below. One by one the birds nestled into the dark figure's body. Finally, they were joined by another bird, an orange bird.

The figure turned to see the orange bird attach itself into his forearm. He gripped his fingers into a fist and then released them. Then he stepped between the twin swords that were stuck into the ground before him. When he reached for them, they glowed at his touch. He dislodged them and twirled them around, striking them together. The swords illuminated and hummed upon contact. He paused for a moment to contemplate his bearings.

With the two swords in his grip, the Crowman began his trek, striding down the path toward the church.